Lock Down Publications and Ca$h
Presents

I0664156

The Lane 2

Written By
KEN-KEN SPENCE

First Edition 2024

Printed in the United States of America

This is a work of fiction. Names, characters, places, and incidents either are products of the author's imagination or are used fictitiously. Any similarity to actual events or locales or persons, living or dead, is entirely coincidental.

Lock Down Publications
P.O. Box 944
Stockbridge, GA 30281
www.lockdownpublications.com

Like our page on Facebook: Lock Down Publications
www.facebook.com/lockdownpublications.ldp

Stay Connected with Us!

Text **LOCKDOWN** to 22828 to stay up-to-date with new releases, sneak peaks, contests and more…

Like our page on Facebook:
Lock Down Publications

Join Lock Down Publications/The New Era Reading Group

Visit our website:
www.lockdownpublications.com

Follow us on Instagram:
Lock Down Publications

Email Us: We want to hear from you!

Dedication

As always I want to thank our Creator for giving me the talent to craft these hood tales. To the memory of my two best friends Christopher (Lil Chris) Pitts and Brandon (8-Dub) McKeller, my happiness ain't the same without you two niggas here with me to share it.

Also, I should have did this in the first book. How could I mention The Lane without giving a shout out to my Lil Nigga? REST IN PEACE MO3!

LONG LIVE THE MANDINGOS

A Note To The Readers

Thank you for buying this book or reading it. I enjoy doing this shit. I wish we could all get together on some beach, smoke a few blunts and have a few drinks but, unfortunately, I have been arrested, convicted of murder and lynched to serve a life sentence by the state of Texas. I'm fighting for my freedom with every word I type in these books.

If you like the book, give me some feedback. I need some muthafuckin mail!

Oh yeah, my address has changed.

Kendall Spence #1594392
Michael Unit
P.O. Box 660400
Dallas, Texas 75266-0400

I hope you enjoy the book.

Ken Ken

Chapter 1

In Houston Robert was going by the name of MOB Rob. At the present time he was laying long dick to Gwen, Big Mack's baby mama. She'd come running right to him after Big Mack was found dead at the hotel.

"Oh shit, you hurting this pussy!" Gwen screamed, throwing it back at him.

"Take this dick like the bad bitch you say you is."

"I'm taking it. I'm taking it, daddy. Oh shit, I'm about to cum all over that dick."

"Let that shit out," he told her, pounding into her pussy like a mad man. "I'm finna nut, too."

"Cum in this pussy, daddy. Oh shit, I feel it. I feel it. I'm cumming, daddy. Fuck me harder! Long stroke this pussy. Yes, yes, yes, I'm cumming. Oh shit, I'm cumming."

"Damn, Gwen, you got some good ass pussy," he told her after he had recovered and caught his breath.

"You got some good ass dick, nigga."

"Now tell me everything that's done happened down there in Dallas," he said reaching over on the nightstand and getting a Newport. He fired it up and took a long drag.

"Like I told you, the laws got Mack for a pistol case and put a federal hold on him. He made some kind of deal with them to get some of those girls that hang out over there on the Lane to testify on that New Orleans nigga that killed Kels and they let him out. Short Dogg found out about it and all hell broke loose.

"They started talking about killing Short Dogg. Fred told them they were snitching and that he was riding with Short Dogg, so Murda killed him in Shalika's house. Kim's truck blew up with all her girls in it. Then one morning we woke up and found Lil' Johnny playing with Murda head. They had killed him and chopped his head off and broke in my shit while we were sleep and put his head in my muthafuckin' apartment.

"We got the fuck up outta there and came down here. We got a room at that hotel. Mack went out to the ice machine to get some ice and sodas and never came back. I went out to check on him about twenty minutes later and found him shot dead by the coke machine."

"Who knew y'all came down here?"

"Nobody. That's what got me puzzled. Nobody knew we came to Houston. Short Dogg didn't follow us way down here. I don't know what the fuck happened."

"These niggas down here real grimy. Somebody probably tried to rob the nigga, and you know how Mack is; he ain't coming off his shit."

"I don't know what happened. I know it's too many muthafuckas done died in the last month. Short Dogg didn't have to kill Murda like that. They supposed to be homeboys."

"Didn't you just say they started talking about killing him first?"

"Yeah, they did."

"Well, what the fuck he supposed to do; let them kill him? Your rat ass baby daddy knows he ain't supposed to be working with the laws on nothing. Murda dumb ass gon' ride with whatever Mack do or say, and Kim a shiesty bitch. I wouldn't put nothing past her pussy-sucking ass."

"What we gon' do? We can't let that nigga Short Dogg get away with this shit."

He grabbed another Newport and got out of bed and went over to the dresser and dipped the Newport in a bottle of wet— embalming fluid— gorilla piss, click-em-juice, or whatever you wanted to call it and lit it up. He took several long, slow pulls on it and blew the smoke out across the room. He immediately started tripping. Gwen turned into a monster and he started laughing. "Damn that shit good," he said getting a hard on again. "Let me fuck you in that big ass booty."

"Hell naw, nigga, you ain't finna put all that dick in my ass."

"Stop acting like a lame ass hoe. You know you want this dick so stop all that frontin'."

"You better go slow."

"Shut the fuck up and get on your knees down here on the edge of the bed." He put his dick in her pussy and stroked her a few times to lube his dick up, then he pulled it out and eased it in her asshole.

"Oh shit, go slow. That shit hurts but it feels good, too."

He eased in her until he was buried inside her. Then he started slow-stroking her. After a while the effects of the wet and her tight, hot ass had him feeling like superman. He started pounding her asshole out like a mad man.

"Oh shit, Robert, it hurts like hell, slow down!" She screamed.

He was zoned out, pounding in her ass like a maniac. Gwen tried to run but he grabbed her around the waist and pinned her to the bed. She was screaming at the top of her lungs.

Lil' Johnny was pounding on the door. "Mama, what's wrong?" he said, starting to cry.

Robert continued to pound her ass until she couldn't take it anymore. She shat all over him. He was so zoned out he didn't even notice. He pounded her until he nutted.

He pulled out a Newport and dipped it and lit it up. He took a few drags and started laughing so hard he was crying.

Gwen was curled up on the bed, her asshole and stomach were on fire. She couldn't move, she was in so much pain.

After Robert got finished smoking, he went over to the bed still laughing and started eating her ass out, shit and all. When she tried to push him away, he went into a zone and punched her in the face, breaking her jaw. He went in a rage and beat her to death while laughing.

Lil' Johnny was at the door beating and crying. He snatched the door open and beat Lil' Johnny to death. He finally laid down on the hallway floor out of breath and laughing while riding his wave. He started laughing out in melodies to the beats of rap songs that were playing in his mind.

After his high came down he got up off the floor and noticed that he was covered in blood. He went into the bedroom and saw the dead bodies of Gwen and Lil' Johnny. "Damn, I fucked up again." He vaguely remembered what he did. "I gotta clean this shit up and get the fuck outta here."

He burned the bodies in a huge drum by pouring gasoline on them. He stayed there all-night pouring gas on the bodies until they were ashes. He went back to the house and got all the bloody sheets and clothes and burned them also.

He started packing the things that he was going to take with him. He noticed an overnight bag that Gwen had brought with her, unzipped it and looked inside. It was full of hundred-dollar bills. It was two hundred and eighty thousand dollars inside the bag.

He put everything in his car and went back in and doused the house with gas and set it on fire. Then, he went and got a hotel room.

After he was settled inside, he thought about smoking another stick of the wet but decided against it because he didn't want to trip out again. Instead, he called his plug and told him that he wanted to buy ten gallons of wet. They set a price and an hour later he was on his way to meet the plug at his spot.

"What up, MOB Rob?" Blow said letting him in the spot.

"Ain't shit, bro. I'm about to head back to Dallas and wanted something to take with me so I could set up shop when I got back," Rob said looking around and noticing that Blow was the only one at the spot.

"What, you gone for good or you coming back?"

"Naw, I'm coming back. I'm just going to the house for a minute. I haven't seen the fam in months."

"I know how that is. A nigga gotta stay in touch with the fam."

Blow went to the closet and took out ten gallons. When he turned around Rob shot him six times in the face. He went to the closet and looked in and saw that it was about two hundred and fifty gallons inside. He loaded the shit up in his trunk and backseat and took off.

Chapter 2

Short Dogg pulled up to Winfield's Hamburgers in two trucks with his whole team. Zell, Shalika, Danielle, K-Rock, J-Low and Em. He'd promised Zell that when they got back from the cruise he would take her to his old hood and get her one of the biggest hamburgers in the city.

They went inside, ordered, and sat at two of the tables in the back and ate. Neither one of them could finish the whole burger.

As they were coming out, two young teenagers ran up on Short Dogg with guns and said, "Run them pockets cuz."

For a minute he just looked at them and smiled. "You know who I am?"

"Yeah, a meal ticket and I'm starving, nigga. Run them pockets." The smallest one said.

"I'm OG Short Dogg."

"Oh shit, we fucked up," the biggest one said taking off running. The lil' nigga hadn't even noticed that he had three guns pointed at him.

"Give me that gun." Short Dogg took the gun from the nigga's hand. "Who your people is, lil' nigga?"

"My mama is Red Tina and my brothers is Yogi and Riff Raff."

"Boy, get yo lil' young ass in the car." He looked over at his crew and told them, "I know this nigga whole family. Let's ride." Short Dogg then asked, "Where Tiger at?"

"That's my daddy; he locked up."

"I know that's your daddy. What's your name?"

"My name is lil' Robert but everybody calls me Smurf."

Short Dogg grew up with Red Tina and Tiger. He'd heard that Tiger had gotten locked up on a murder case a couple of months ago. But he didn't know if he was back on the streets yet. Tiger had already beat two or three murder cases over the last few years.

Tiger had started a Deuce Deuce Beckley Crip set on Alaska Street in the hood. They had an ongoing war going with the Crips from Glendale. Short Dogg was beloved in their hood because everybody knew that he went to Glendale and smoked several of their homies after one of them killed one of his OG's at a house party.

They pulled up on the block and it was niggas sitting out on porches and ducked off in cars, watching everything and everybody that came on the street. The Glendale niggas had been doing drive-bys on the block almost every other night.

They pulled up at the corner house and Short Dogg saw Yogi and Riff Raff sitting on the porch. They all got out the car.

"Short Dogg, what's up homie?" Riff Raff greeted him.

"What up bro?" Yogi said.

"Ain't shit. Where Red Tina at?" Short Dogg asked.

"She in the house. What this lil' nigga done did?" Yogi asked.

"Oh, him and his lil' partner tried to stick a nigga up at Winfield's."

Short Dogg and Zell went inside to talk to Red Tina, the house was littered with drug paraphernalia, and it was six or seven people stuffing their pipes with crack and firing up. A pretty little girl about three or four years old was sitting on the couch, watching cartoons.

"Baby, we gotta get these kids outta here," Zell said.

"I was thinking the same thing. But, I can't see myself putting CPS on Red Tina. Her and my mama was cool and went to school together."

"I wasn't thinking about CPS. Let's take them with us."

"If that's what you want to do, I'm with it. Let's find Red Tina and get the hell outta here. That crack smoke stinks." Short Dogg asked the little girl, "Where yo' mama at?"

"She in the back room. I'll go get her." She jumped off the couch and a few minutes later came back with Red Tina.

"Omar, boy, what the hell is you doing in my house. I ain't seen you since Lil' Chris funeral." Red Tina was one of the baddest chicks in the hood. Even though she smoked crack it didn't diminish her beauty or her body. She was still thick and pretty.

"Let me take these kids outta this area and put them in school out there where I stay. Lil' Robert just tried to rob me at Winfield's."

"Did Faye put you up to this? She been telling me to get them outta this area for the last year. Now, they got this shit going on with them fools from Glendale. They shot my damn house up last week; almost hit my baby, Shayla." She said pointing at the little girl. "Where you gonna take my kids to?"

"We stay in Prosper."

"This the girl I met at the funeral that you was gonna marry? Did y'all ever get married?"

Zell held up her finger.

"Let me go get you they social security cards and birth certificates. You gonna need all that to check them in school. Shayla, come back here and get your clothes together."

Shayla and Smurf packed the little clothes they had and Short Dogg gave Red Tina all his contact information and they left.

Before they got in the car, Riff Raff pulled Short Dogg over and told him, "Bro, I appreciate this. We been trying to get them away from here while we got this war going on with them niggas."

"We from the hood, nigga. You know I got you. Y'all need to stop playing with them niggas and get at they OG's. Every time one of them niggas come out the house, be waiting in the bushes. Them niggas will get they shit together and forget about beefing," Short Dogg told him.

"We got some shit planned for they ass that's gonna rock they world."

"Alright, y'all handle them niggas. Let me get my people outta here."

"Alright. One." They shook hands and Short Dogg got in the truck and they left.

Chapter 3

The next day Short Dogg was all about business. They got Shayla and Smurf settled in their own rooms and put their things away. He'd called Faye and told her that he had Red Tina's two youngest kids. When he left the house, Danielle and the kids were on-line shopping for things they didn't need.

He was with Em and K-Rock and they were on their way to one of his sports bars where he was meeting with his brothers, Dub and Big Dre. Short Dogg and Big Dre wanted to get out the game. But the whole team wasn't set up financially like they needed to be before they could leave the game. Plus, they'd met a plug while on the cruise, and Glenn had talked the Colombian into some prices they couldn't pass up.

They met Enrique while chilling and drinking at one of the bars on the ship. They small talked about where they were from and what type of work they did. Short Dogg told him that he owned a few sports bars and clubs. Enrique was born in Colombia but had been in America most of his life. His mother was a Mexican American and his father was Colombian; at the present time he was living in Florida.

The next day at the same bar, Enrique walked up and shook Short Dogg's hand. "I did some checking on you last night and it seems we have mutual friends."

"Checking on me? I'm not that interesting or that important."

"No, my friend, it seems that you are a very important person to a man in my line of business. You have the reputation of being a standup guy. A very respected and trusted guy in business."

"What line of business are you in?"

"Import, export; that sort of thing."

"Who is our mutual friend?'

"Rudy Martinez."

"Yeah, I know Rudy."

"He speaks highly of you. I can make you a very rich man. I have connections everywhere. Judges, Senators, Chief of Police, Mayors, Governors and every street corner or city you can think of."

"If you know Rudy, I'm sure he told you that I'm recently married and recently retired."

"I met your beautiful wife, Zell, at the gym earlier this morning. Let me ask you this. You may be financially secure but is your team in the same position as you are? I'm aware that you have had some recent problems with some of your team. But you have weeded most of the trash out. This mob thing you created is a cartel of its own. Now, let me show you how to take it from a street gang to an empire. I'm going to take you from a street king to a kingpin. The first thing you need to do is forget about that street gang non-sense and turn it into a family or cartel."

Short Dogg had been thinking about all that Enrique said. He was sure with the right people in place he could make millions and never become the target of any law agency. He'd already told Enrique five years and he was through.

They got to the sports bar and went in through the backdoor. Everyone was already there when they arrived.

"Okay, as y'all already know, we back in the game. We have five years to get our money right. If your money ain't right in five years, that's your fault. I'm gone for good in five years, no exceptions. The MOB is no longer a blood gang. We are now a crime family and anybody that can help the growth of our distribution will be added to the team. I will no longer answer to Short Dogg. My name is Omar. Glenn, you are over the white girl. Jay, you are over the green. Dre, you are over the brown. Dell, you are over the meth, and Dub, you are over the pills. Each one of you has three days to set up a base of where you will be operating from so I can have your product delivered to you. For now, Dub, you can use our old apartment. We haven't been in there since Chris died. Em, you are my personal assistant and you and the girls are over security."

The next couple of weeks were spent getting their people organized and trying to secure spots so that they could cook, bag and cut their work up.

Enrique called and saved the day. "Omar, I have a house that would be perfect for you. I'm flying into the city in a couple of days. Meet me and I will show you the house."

"Okay, call me when you get here."

Chapter 4

Robert made it to Dallas and went straight to the Lane. He drove up and down the block seeing some familiar faces and some new ones. They had told him about the changes over the phone, but he wasn't prepared to see a security booth in front of the Bent Creek Apartments.

He drove up to the corner store and parked in the parking lot. There were people posted up as usual. Niggas was hustling, selling sacks of weed, x-pills, crack and powder. Some niggas were selling CD's and movies. He just sat back in the car and watched.

Rob felt comfortable being back in the hood he grew up in. He went to Houston to try and get his rap career going, nationally. But on a local level he was a legend on the Lane. He'd gained stardom when he dropped the hood anthem *That's Our Block*. Right to this day, you couldn't have a party on Forest Lane or any surrounding area without hearing:

Forest Lane, that's our block
Get to bullshittin' we'll knock you out ya socks
We don't give a fuck
Cause the heat stay cocked
Yeahhhh
Forest Lane nigga
That's our block

Or the street banger, *Lane Baby*.

He went to Houston after the success of his mixtape to try and make it big. So far he'd only been able to make a few mixtapes that did alright and hop on a few remixes with some artist who had songs on the radio. Things weren't moving fast enough for him. He didn't understand that he was building his brand with the mixtapes and features. He wanted overnight success and when that didn't happen, he got impatient and started back to smoking wet.

He saw a familiar face. A MOB rat chick named Lisa that the whole hood had fucked numerous times. He watched her as she went in the store and came back out. She stood around for a few minutes talking to some of the hustlers before she took off walking. He started his car and followed her out the parking lot. He followed her down the Lane until she turned into the Palms Apartments. He turned in behind her and pulled up on the side of her and hit the horn.

"Lisa," he said, rolling his window down.

"Who dat is?" she said walking over to the car, looking inside. "Oh shit, Robert, that's you." She hugged him through the window.

"What's up baby girl? Get in and come fuck with me for a minute."

"Come to the spot. Bobi and D-Money got a spot back here and they ain't seen you in a couple of years. You are family. Let's go kick it."

"Naw, I don't want them niggas to know I'm back yet. I'ma park right here. Go get us a sack of Dro', and let's go chill." He handed her a $50 bill.

"I gotta take these cigars and Newports up there anyway. Stay right here and I'll be back in about five or ten minutes." She took the money and walked off.

He watched her as she walked off and said to himself, "Damn, her ass still fat."

Lisa was twenty-two, no kids, honey complected, cute face with big breasts, small waist and a dump truck ass. If she didn't fuck every nigga with a hard dick, she would have been a bad bitch. But, with her reputation and baggage she was just another hood rat bitch.

When she came back and got in, Rob drove straight to the Icebox on Skillman and loaded up on liquor. He bought Vodka, Patron, Gin, Hennessey and some Crown Royal. "You want something in particular?" He asked her.

"Naw. You know me, I'm straight up outta the hood. I'll drink whatever."

"Oh shit, I almost forgot. Get a case of Bud Ice."

While she went and got the beer he went and got plastic cups, Coke and Red Bull. At the counter he got two cartons of Newports, a box of cigars and some cherry incense. He paid for the stuff and they left.

A black Benz pulled up on the side of him and honked. "Robert, when you get back in town?" A light skinned nigga asked getting out of the car.

"J-Don, what up blood? I just got back today. What you been up to?"

"Man, you know me. Still pimping these hos and selling pounds of that Kush on the side. What's up, Lisa? You ain't gon' speak?"

"Hey, J-Don," she said getting in the car and closing the door.

"That's a real live hustling ass bitch. I been trying to get her to stop giving her pussy away for free and let me sell it for her."

"I'ma see if she really ready to take the next step. My nigga, I got some gallons of that Dip for the low-low. You know anybody that fuck around?"

"Is the shit good?"

"Nigga, ain't nothing changed about me. You know I don't sell no bunk shit. This shit fresh from Cali and it's that click-em-juice."

"Give me your number and I'll hit you up. Let me check with some of my niggas."

"What them pounds going for?" He asked while putting his number in J-Don's phone.

"I'll let you get one for thirty-two hundred."

"You got one of them joints on you right now?"

"Yeah, I got one in the car."

"Let me get this bread out the car. I'ma fuck with you on one of them." He got in the car and counted out the money for him. J-Don came to the car and handed him the pound wrapped in a sack and he gave him the money. "I'ma call you tomorrow and let you know something on that wet."

"Alright, get at me," Robert said, pulling off.

"That shit got the whole car lit up," Lisa said, talking about the weed he'd bought from J-Don.

"That shit gotta be some fire as loud as it is."

"He known for having that good. The nigga always at the Ice Box selling pounds."

"Tell me what the fuck been going on down here. Kim dead, Murda dead, Fred dead, Big Mack dead—"

"Big Mack and Gwen left town after Murda got killed."

"Big Mack dead. Somebody killed that nigga in Houston at a hotel. Now Gwen and Lil' Johnny missing."

"Damn, that's the first I heard about Big Mack. Them niggas was on some grimy shit. Mack and Murda was robbing and murdering all over the hood. From what I heard, them niggas started trippin' with Short Dogg. They shot a few of his workers and spots up. The next thing I knew Murda was dead and Kim was dead. I very seldom see Short Dogg anymore in the hood."

"I wouldn't come to the hood either. That nigga put the whole hood on and that's the thanks he get, betrayal." Robert said.

"Kim was a no good bitch. I'm sure she orchestrated all that grimy shit. I been saw through her fake ass. That's why I never joined her little clique. I'm MOB all day but I ain't with her little female clique."

"What started all the bullshit?"

"From what I heard, Big Mack made some kind of deal with the laws to get them hos that hang with Kim to testify on the nigga who shot and killed Lil' Kels. Short Dogg found out about it and told them they was foul."

"So them niggas went to trippin' with Short Dogg 'cause he told them fools the real?"

"That's what the word is."

"So, why the niggas kill Fred?"

"'Cause Fred told them the same thing Short Dogg told them: that they were wrong and if they went at Short Dogg with some drama, he was riding with him and they had to come at him too. So, they killed him."

"Coward muthafuckas."

He was really just making conversation and trying to check the story that Gwen had told him. He was sure that he had the real truth about what happened now that Lisa basically told him the same thing Gwen did.

He drove to the Comforter Suites in Carrollton and paid for a room for a month.

Chapter 5

Omar and Enrique stood in the foyer of the five-million-dollar home in the Preston Hollow area of Dallas. It had two guest houses, a small house at the front of the property that would house the person who manned the electric gate that allowed entrance to the property, indoor and outdoor swimming pools, eight car garage, 12 bedrooms, 15 bathrooms and 8 fireplaces. The property was secluded with the closest neighbors being a nice distance away. Omar fell in love with the home and decided that he wanted to live in the house. He would give his mom and pops his house, move to this new house and use their house as a stash spot for his drugs.

"You like this home, huh?"

"This is the baddest house I have ever seen."

"It's yours. You move your family here, give your place to your moms and use her house as your base."

Damn, I hate it when this old man reads my mind, he thought. "Yeah, that's what I was thinking." He said out loud.

"Here," he said, throwing Omar the keys to the place and several fobs to open the electric gate with. "Oh yeah, I almost forgot," he said, handing him a small envelope. "That is the key and address to the storage where your package is. It's a safe place but I would have it all outta there within the next thirty days. You don't want to have too much traffic at that place."

"I'll go check it out first thing in the morning."

"Well, son, I got a plane to catch. I'm going home for a couple of months. Call me if you need me."

"Alright."

They shook hands and Enrique got back in the car with his driver and left.

Omar locked the house up and got in his car and drove home. He called his mom and pops and told them to meet him at his house. When he got home his mom and pops were waiting on him. "I'm giving y'all this house."

"Boy, you just bought this damn house. Zell ain't finna move out of this house," Faye said, looking over at Zell who had just walked in and caught the last of the conversation.

"I love this house. Omar and Danielle and Shalika does too."

"Baby, just trust me. I got us a new house I promise you will love. Ma, I need y'all to start packing. I need y'all outta that house by the weekend."

"What the hell you got going on? I would love to have this house but you ain't finna have Zell mad at me and pops."

Pops was just sitting back listening. He already knew what the deal was with Enrique and he knew that if Omar was giving them his house he had something bigger and better.

"Okay, shit. Danielle, Shalika, Em, y'all get in here." He called out. "Baby, get everybody down here." When Em came in the room, he said, "Get two of the Suburbans ready and tell J-Low and K-Rock to come on. We finna take a ride. Danielle, get Shayla and Smurf so we can take this ride."

Pops drove his truck with Danielle and the kids and the rest of them piled into the two Suburbans and they drove back out to the house. It was dark by the time they got back.

As they got close, Omar could see lights on through the windows. "The lights must come on automatically when it gets dark. I know I turned the lights off before I left."

"Omar, is this the house?" Zell asked as he pulled the fob out of his pocket and opened the gates. "This is beautiful. I love it already. What you think, Shalika?"

"I'm speechless. Look how big it is."

"I told you to trust me." Omar said smiling. As they pulled in front of the house, Omar saw two cars parked in the driveway. "I wonder who this is."

Before they could all get out the cars, the front door opened and a tall, slim, Mexican lady stepped out drying her hands on a towel. "Hello, you must be Omar and you are Zell and Shalika." She said in a heavy accent.

"Yes, we are. Who are you?"

"I am Marie, the maid and housekeeper. My husband, Antonio, is the cook, my two sons Victor and Pablo are the grounds keepers, and their wives Jessica and Mary are the nannies. Enrique says that we are all fired if you have hired your own people. If not, we would be happy to serve you and your family."

He looked over at Zell and Shalika and nodded. "Well, Marie, you can start your new job by showing us around the house. This is my mom Faye, my father Pops, this is Kelly, Michelle and Jasmine, and this is our daughter—"

"Danielle. Enrique told us all about her. The little ones?"

"This is Robert and Shayla."

"Come, let me show you around the house."

She took them around and showed them the house, and Zell and Shalika were in love. Danielle had already picked her room and Shayla's too. Marie showed them the basement where there was a maid quarters, with three bedrooms and four bathrooms, kitchen and living room. There was a pool house that was the size of a small home and another guest house in the back of the property that Omar hadn't seen earlier when he was with Enrique.

The house had two wings— the east and west— each with six bedrooms. The west wing was the biggest and Zell chose that wing for the family to live. Em, K-Rock and J-Low went to the east wing to pick out their bedrooms while Omar, Zell and Shalika went to the west wing. Danielle, Shayla and Smurf were already somewhere on the west wing exploring. Faye and Pops were still with Marie checking out the rest of the house.

"This is the master suite," Zell said as they stepped into one of the bedrooms. "It has two bathrooms and four closets. Look how big these closets are."

"This is almost as big as my old apartment," Shelika said.

"We have to christen this room," Zell said.

"We'll come back tomorrow without my mom and pops," Omar said knowing Zell wanted some dick.

"Shalika, lock the bedroom door. Come on, Omar, it'll be perfectly fine. The door is locked," she said, grabbing his crotch. "See, it's already getting hard." Zell undid his pants, pulled his dick out and stuck it down her throat. "Come on, Shalika. I need some help with this thing." Just like that Shalika was on her knees and they were both sharing his dick.

"Fuck this shit. I'm finna fuck the shit out of both of you," Omar said, pulling them up. "Pull them pants down," he told them while stroking his dick. When they pulled their pants off, he dropped down and licked both of their pussies. He had to lick Zell's from the back because her stomach was stuck out so far at seven months pregnant. "Both of y'all pussies are already wet. Did y'all plan this shit?"

"Our pussies stay wet," Shalika said.

He bent Zell over and Shalika grabbed his dick and guided it into Zell. She sucked and licked all over Zell's breast while he fucked her.

"Oh shit, Omar, I'm gonna cum. Hit it harder. Yeah, just like that," she said as he started banging her back out. "I'm cumming. I'm cumming all over your dick, Omar."

"Let that shit out, baby."

"It won't stop. I'm cumming again." Finally after she stopped nutting, she pulled off his dick and stumbled to the floor. "Your turn, Shalika."

Shalika dropped down and sucked Zell's juices off his dick before she stood up and bent over so he could put his dick in her. He started out fucking her slow while Zell cheered him on. "Cum in her pussy. Give her all that dick."

"Yes, yes, fuck this pussy. Make me cum all over that dick. I feel it in my stomach. Hurt that pussy, baby. Beat it up. Fuck me hard."

He started pounding her back out. When he saw Zell get up and French kiss Shalika, he lost it and shot a gallon of cum up her pussy. They came at the same time.

After they got dressed and were getting ready to leave the room, Shalika said, "Good thing we got two nannies. I'm pregnant, too."

"How do you know?" Zell asked excitedly.

"I got a test from the store about two weeks ago."

"Why you didn't say something?" Omar asked.

"I was waiting for the right moment."

"Okay, can we all agree not to keep secrets from each other about things like this? I'm going to be a father; I need to know things like that as soon as you know."

"We are all going to be one big happy family. I can't wait to have this little girl so we can get started on another one," Zell said, hugging Shalika.

"Who said we were having another one?" He asked playfully.

"I'm not taking birth control and we are not going to stop fucking, so we are more likely than not going to have another baby or two."

"Yep, we both are," Shalika said, getting in on the game.

They went back downstairs where Pops and Faye were in the living room smoking a big ass blunt.

"Where y'all get that good?" Omar asked.

"Yo nasty ass would know if you and them girls wouldn't have been up there fucking. Y'all been married too long to still be fucking like teenagers. Yo nasty ass too, Shalika," Faye said, hitting the blunt.

"Ma, you tripping, we ain't been doing nothing like that. We been up there checking out the rooms." Omar lied.

"Boy, stop lying," Faye said.

"Where y'all get the weed?"

"From Marie, your housekeeper."

"Um, excuse me, Mama Faye, but your dress on inside out and it wasn't like that a while ago."

"Ma, what you and Pops been doing in my house?"

"Shut yo nasty ass up. I had to use the bathroom."

"You had to get naked?" Zell asked.

Pops just sat there with a sheepish ass grin on his face, high as hell from the weed they'd gotten from Marie.

"Let's get the hell out of here so we can start packing," Omar said.

Chapter 6

Omar was at the storage with his brothers Big Dre and Dub. They were all in shock. Inside the storage was two thousand bricks of cocaine, two thousand bricks of heroin, two thousand bricks of meth, five million mollies and x-pills, and ten thousand pounds of vacuum sealed weed.

"Man, this Columbian is crazy," Omar said.

"We big time now, baby bro," Glenn answered, ready to get started moving the shit.

"We are going to be moving this shit outta here in a week or two so y'all get what you will need for a couple of weeks so we won't have to keep running back and forth to this storage."

Jay took about 25 pounds of weed, Dub took about a million pills, Big Dre took about 30 bricks of the brown, Dell took 25 bricks of the meth, and Glenn took 50 bricks of cocaine.

Dub had already been networking. He went to every club and bar and talked to all the DJs, bartenders and bouncers and told them that he had the pills for three dollars apiece if they bought a hundred or more. His phone was ringing off the hook. In twenty-four hours he had already sold over a hundred thousand pills.

Big Dre ran through the thirty bricks he had so fast he had to call Omar four days later to tell him he needed thirty more. Jay sold the whole twenty-five pounds to a nigga he knew in Oklahoma. He needed to visit the storage the next day. Omar was heated that he had to keep going to the storage, but he was happy to see that his team was on their shit and moving the product. Dell split his twenty-five bricks between two people who actually wanted twenty-five apiece, so he was calling Omar to let him back in the storage two days later also.

Glen had customers coming from every state you could think of. When he called his people and told them his prices and hours, he had niggas on their way to Texas from New Mexico, Georgia, Louisiana, Michigan, Mississippi, Nebraska, Alabama, Tennessee, Kansas and Missouri. In 72 hours, Glenn and his team had already moved almost a thousand bricks.

The money was coming in fast, and everything was going smooth. Omar and his family had made the move to the new house and Faye, Pops and Junior had made the move to Omar's old house. The team made the move to Faye's old house. Zell and Shalika spent most of their time online shopping for art and furniture to decorate the new home.

Omar was at the spot counting money with Junior and Glenn when he got a call from Yogi. "What's the deal?" Omar answered.

"Bro, I need you to get Smurf and Shayla and bring them out to Baylor Hospital. Man, them fuck niggas got us last night," he said, his voice cracking up.

"What happened?"

"Bro, them niggas got Raff and they shot up Red Tina and everybody in the house."

"Raff and Red Tina alright?"

"Raff dead, my nigga, and Mama in critical condition. They don't think she gone make it."

"Fam, I'm on my way to the house to get them and we'll meet you at the hospital in a few."

"The lil' nigga gonna take this real hard."

"We'll talk in a few. You just keep yourself together."

"Alright, one."

"One."

Omar told Gleen what happened and then he called Zell and Shalika and told them to get the kids ready and meet him at the hospital. He called Faye and told her and Dub, D-Money and Bobi. By the time he got to the hospital the whole hood was there. It was more than two hundred people inside or standing around outside waiting on some kind of news on how Red Tina was doing and showing their support for the homie Riff Raff.

Zell and Shalika came over to him when they saw he had made it and told him that Yogi had took the kids in to see Red Tina.

"How did he take it?" Omar asked.

"He took it really well. But Shayla cried a little. I don't think she really understands what's going on," Zell answered.

"Shits about to get real hectic in the hood."

"I hope she's alright."

They stood around talking for a few minutes waiting on some kind of news from the doctors about Red Tina. She was in surgery, fighting for her life.

Omar finally got a chance to talk to Yogi. "What happened?"

"Bro, they got us good. We were all on the block chilling and hustling when three cars came by and hit the block up. We started shooting back. Five minutes after those three cars left, three more came by and started shooting. Every time one car would leave, another three would show up. Eventually we ran out of bullets and had to run in the house. That's when they started hitting the house up. I think they got Riff Raff on that first volley. After they finally got through shooting, I found him laying on the side of the house. He'd been hit about six times, and he was already gone. Then, they started screaming and hollering in the house that Mama was hit so I ran to the house and she was in the back room with blood all over her head and chest."

"Did they let Smurf see her when y'all went up?"

"Naw, the doctor or nurse or whatever she is was explaining that she had a gunshot wound to the head and three to the torso and that she was in surgery."

"Man, this shit is crazy. The whole hood is gonna ride for Riff Raff and Red Tina. Them niggas fucked up when they did that."

"It was bodies everywhere. The lil' nigga that was with Smurf when they tried to rob you got killed too. It's like five people dead and like twelve to fifteen people got shot. We gotta get at them niggas, bro, and hit them niggas hard. I can't let this ride. Them niggas killed my brother, my nigga. I'ma ride for Riff until I'm dead or all them niggas dead. Ain't no peace treaties or no making up. If any nigga from the hood even come to me talking about a peace treaty I'ma smoke him, too."

While they were talking the doctor came out and called Yogi and the immediate family away. They walked out of the waiting room and seconds later they all heard Yogi yell, "Hell naw! They killed my Mama! Them niggas killed my Mama!"

Omar looked over at Smurf and he was being consoled by Em, J-Low and K-Rock. But he was dry-eyed and not showing any emotion at all. He was just nodding to whatever they were telling him. Shayla was crying but that was only because she saw her big brother and other family members crying.

Faye finally showed up and Omar told her that one of her best friends was gone. She was a veteran of hood wars and beef, so she knew the life and what the outcome would more than likely be. She grew up burying her homeboys and homegirls lost in gang wars and hood beefs. But she still took the loss of her homegirl Red Tina hard.

"All the shit we went through growing up and all the close calls we had and made it out to be almost middle-aged women for her to lose her life like this is hard to deal with.

This is some shit she didn't even have nothing to do with," Faye said.

When they finally got ready to go, they couldn't find Smurf anywhere. They searched all over the hospital, but he was nowhere to be found.

"Yogi, you seen Smurf?" Omar asked.

"Naw, he was over there with them lil' niggas about ten minutes ago," he said pointing.

Omar looked over there where he pointed and the area was empty.

"Man, them lil' niggas took off. I hope that little crazy ass nigga ain't went to go do no dumb shit," Yogi said.

Omar called his phone several times, but it kept going to voicemail. Omar already knew Smurf was about to ride for his moms and big brother, and it was nothing he could do about it.

Chapter 7

Robert and Lisa were smoking a Newport dipped in wet, high as fuck and laughing. They'd been drinking and smoking all night. He looked over at Lisa and she turned into a monster. He reached over and slapped the shit out of her. Lisa never stopped laughing. She calmly reached over, grabbed the bottle of vodka, and took a long drink. Then, she hit him across the head with the bottle all the while still laughing.

Robert was knocked unconscious. When he woke up, he was tied to the bed and Lisa was still laughing while dancing around the room naked, smoking a Newport dipped in his wet. She looked over and saw that he was awake and danced over to him and put the cigarette in his mouth. He took a long drag and inhaled the smoke, immediately feeling the chemicals relax his body. He started laughing.

She hauled off and slapped the shit out of him, then whispered in his ear, "If you ever put your hands on me again, I'ma kill you." She said it in the sweetest, kindest, gentlest voice he'd ever heard.

His heart burst open and he felt emotions he'd never felt in his life. He was instantly in love with her. He nodded, in love with her gangsta.

She leaned over and stared him in his eyes for a long time as if she was reading his soul from his eyes. He was hooked; he couldn't look away. She kissed him long and hard. He felt himself getting hard with an animal lust he'd never felt. She started laughing when she saw his hard dick. She caressed it and stroked it until it was as hard as it would ever get. Then, she started giving him the best head he'd ever had.

She started out slow and paid attention to every inch of his dick. When he finally released his nut, it was like the floodgates opened. He must have shot a gallon of nut down her throat. She swallowed every drop. She got on top of him and rode his face to four orgasms.

Robert really wasn't a pussy eating nigga, but he ate her pussy out and couldn't get enough of her taste and smell. She looked down at him and saw that his face was covered in her juices. She started laughing and licked every drop from his face. Then, she climbed on his dick and rode him for an hour straight. They both fell asleep afterwards. When Robert woke up, she was still asleep but she had removed his restraints.

He looked at her sleeping for a moment, kissed her lips and cuddled up next to, her pulling her to him and putting his arms around her. He went back to sleep.

They woke up to Robert's phone going off. He grabbed it off the nightstand and saw that it was J-Don getting back at him. "What's the deal?"

"I'm trying to get two of those gallons. If it's that gorilla piss then my nigga gonna fuck with you on about five or six."

"I'll meet you at the Ice Box in about an hour."

"Alright, one."

"One."

"You just lost almost fifty thousand dollars," Lisa told him.

"Why you say that? I just made twenty thousand."

"I can bottle that shit up and make almost fifty stacks a gallon."

"Yeah, but how long is it gonna take to get off of it and we don't have no spot to sell it at?"

"Just trust me on this and let me show you how to make this money. You are a rapper and I'm the trapper," she said smiling.

"Okay, but uh," Robert started to say, seeming embarrassed.

"But what?"

"But uh, will you marry me?"

Lisa was shocked. She never imagined a nigga wanting to marry her. She knew she had fucked a lot of niggas but she was single and felt like she was enjoying her life. If a man did the same thing it wouldn't be shit said about it. But, when a female did it, they were called hos, thots, bust downs or whatever a nigga could think of. She knew she was a good girl and for the right nigga that would give his all to her, respect her and treat her with love and kindness, she would be committed, dedicated and give him her all. She just didn't want to be lied to, used or heartbroken after she made a commitment. "You ain't gotta marry me to get no pussy."

"That ain't even what this is about. I fell in love with that gangsta shit. The way you handled me and stood up for yourself after I slapped the shit out of you made me feel some kind of way. I can't fuck with no weak ass bitch. I need a gangsta bitch that ain't gone except nothing but the best from a nigga."

"Damn, that shit right there was poetic. You on some real live mack shit without even trying to be," she told him, smiling. "But, I'm feeling that shit you was spitting, and if you really serious I'll marry you. But dig these reds. I been in love one time in my whole life and the nigga fucked my best friend, my sister, my mama and my aunt. Ever since then I been HPD. That's hump, pump, and dumping these niggas. If you fuck over me, Robert, and hurt me, I'ma kill you my nigga, and I'ma chop your dick off and feed it to you first."

"See, that's that gangsta shit I'm talking about. But, I'm not going to fuck over you. I don't do no fake shit. I don't lie just to kick it and I don't do shit halfway. It's all or nothing with me. So, if you ain't ready to give me your all, then don't take my last name. 'Cause if you fuck over me, I'ma be the last thing you ever see in this world."

"Let's do this shit then."

"You damn sure ain't gotta worry about me fucking over you 'cause I ain't ready to eat no dick."

They both burst out laughing. Robert grabbed her and kissed her. He stuck a yard of tongue down her throat. They stayed like that for several minutes before they finally broke the kiss. Lisa hadn't kissed a nigga in over five years.

Chapter 8

Lil' Smurf and six of his little homies were in two stolen old school Monte Carlos, three in each car, two in the front and one in the back. They had been riding the streets every night since they left the hospital hoping to catch them slipping. So far they'd been unlucky.

Smurf pulled out his phone and reread the message that Omar sent him the night he left the hospital. *"Lil nigga, I ain't gon' tell you not to do what you gon' do anyway. If the shoe was on the other foot, I'd be where you at right now too. But what I am gon' tell you is this, handle yo' bidness so I don't have to get my hands dirty. We got Shayla. You just come back when you get it out yo' system. OG.SD."*

Smurf nodded in the darkness of the backseat. He turned the phone off and put it back in his pocket. They were parked on a street where they could watch the traffic coming in and out of Glendale. Just as they were about to drive to the other end of the hood, the city bus pulled up and a girl they all knew got off the bus.

"Hey, that's that nigga OG Mark sister right there," Lil' Paul said from the passenger seat.

"Yeah, that's the bitch," Yaki said in the driver's seat.

"Call them niggas in the other car and tell them to block the bitch off if she try to run. Pull up on the side of her. Hurry up, nigga."

Yaki started the car and pulled up right next to her. Smurf jumped out and tackled the bitch to the ground. He hit her with three or four haymakers that had her discombobulated and yelled over his shoulder, "Help me get the bitch to the car, dumb ass nigga."

"Smurf I ain't got nothing to do with y'all beef." She tried pleading.

"My mama ain't had nothing to do with it either. Take us to the spot on Eisenhower," he told Yaki after they got back in the car.

"Man, what we gon' do with this bitch?" Lil' Paul asked.

Smurf ignored him and continued to stare out the window. All he could think about was his brother and mother. He wanted to kill everything from Glendale.

"Bro, you hear me?" Paul asked.

"My nigga shut the fuck up. I heard you the first time and didn't answer you."

"Who you talking to like that?" Lil' Paul asked, getting heated.

Smurf didn't even bother replying. He just pulled his gun out and blew Lil' Paul's shit all over the dashboard and window.

"What the fuck Smurf!" Yaki said.

"You good my nigga?" Smurf asked him, still holding his pistol.

"Yeah, nigga, I'm good. But bro, you losing yo' mind."

"I lost my mind the day my brother and my mama died."

When they got to the house, the three niggas that were in the other car came over and stared at Lil' Paul's dead body. "What happened to Paul?" CeCe finally asked.

"He had an accident. He talked too much," Smurf answered, continuing to the house. When they got in the house, Smurf was all business. "Call your brother, Trina."

She pulled out her phone and dialed his number. When he answered, she handed the phone to Smurf.

"What's up fuck boy?"

"Who the fuck is this and where Trina at?"

"This is Smurf, and Trina right here with me."

"If you hurt my sister, nigga, I'ma murk everything you love."

"Bitch ass nigga, you already murked everything I love. Now, I'm finna start murking the shit you love." He pulled out his pistol and shot three times on the floor. Then he pushed the end button on the phone. "Y'all get to the block and get the hood ready. Them niggas is on their way. Smoke everything that comes through. Dump that nigga Paul body somewhere on the way. I'ma stay here with Trina."

"You want me to stay here with you, my nigga?" Yaki asked.

"Naw, I'm good my nigga. Hit me up and let me know what happens." Trina's phone was ringing off the hook. He ignored every call. After they left, he told Trina, "You might as well get comfortable. We gonna be here for a while."

"How long you gonna keep me here?"

"Don't start asking me all them dumb ass questions. You lucky you ain't dead, so be thankful."

"I don't have shit to do with all this shooting and killing. All I do is work and go to school and you know it. I'm sorry about your brother and Red Tina. This shit don't have nothing to do with no hood beef. Mark didn't even know they did that shit. Red Tina helped raise all of us. Ain't no way in hell Mark would have let them niggas shoot up Red Tina house. Dee-Man did that shit 'cause he found out that Yogi was fucking Pam. He took all them young niggas with him. That's who did that shit. Dee-Man and them young niggas he keep around him."

"My brother ain't fucking with that bitch Pam so why you trying to spin me with this bullshit?"

"Boy, yo' brother been fucking Pam. She left Dee-Man and started fucking with Yogi almost a year ago. All this recent shit been Yogi and Dee-Man beefing over Pam."

"Did Riff know Yogi was fucking Pam?"

"I don't know. But I doubt it. They stay sneaking around too much."

"How you find out?"

"You know me and Pam is tight. I have rode with them to the motel several times when she was still fucking with Dee-Man 'cause she told him she was with me."

Smurf sat back thinking; he was mad as fuck at Yogi for his betrayal. His mom and brother were dead because of who he was fucking. He wouldn't have been mad if Yogi had told them what the play was. But he was sneaking and doing the shit and then when the shit hit the fan, he still was acting like he didn't know what the fuck was going on. "Call your brother and tell him that you alive and safe so he don't send them niggas to the hood looking for you."

While she was calling her brother, he called Yogi. His phone went to voicemail. He tried back several times and got the same results. He figured he was with Pam and didn't want to be bothered. He told Trina after she got off the phone with her brother to call Pam's phone and see if she answered. Pam answered on the first ring.

"What up, bitch? You in the hood?" Trina asked.

"Naw, I'm way out here in the country somewhere with my baby."

"Who, Dee-Man?"

"Bitch, don't play. You know I'm with Yogi."

"Damn, that nigga don't give you no breaks, do he?"

"Bitch, when you got that snapper a nigga wanna block and lock it down," she said laughing.

"Bitch, you crazy. You sound like you falling in love with this nigga, or is this you just passing time?"

"I'm in love with this nigga for real, girl. He just knows how to treat a woman. I feel important and respected when I'm with him and not just a piece of meat. Don't get it twisted though, this nigga be putting in that work when it's time to get down and dirty. But, it ain't all about that. He listens to me and talks to me and pays attention to me. You know what I'm saying?"

"Yeah, I feel you. I'm happy for you too. What y'all gonna do about all this beefing? These niggas aint gonna let y'all be happy with all this shit going on."

"Ain't nobody really trippin' but that nigga Dee-Man. He just mad 'cause his dumb ass ain't have enough game to hold on to a bitch. The only time I saw that nigga was when he wanted his dick sucked or some pussy. A bitch get tired of that shit."

"I know that's right."

"Bitch, you need to find you a man. You ain't had no dick in almost a year and a half. What's wrong with you? That's why yo' ass so grouchy, you need some dick," Pam said laughing.

"Bitch, dick ain't everything it's made up to be. I don't need no dick to be happy. I need a nigga that treat me like a woman, that listens, pays attention to me and make me feel like a queen."

"Oh shit," Pam moaned on the phone. "Yogi, stop doing that, I'm on the phone."

"What he doing?" Trina asked, being nosey.

"I'ma call you back, Trina, I gotta go." She ended the call.

"I told you that boy in love with that girl," Trina told Smurf.

He sat there thinking about all he heard. He had to admit that Pam was a bad bitch. But Yogi was still out of line for not putting them on guard. "I'm finna lay down and go to sleep. You can call somebody to come get you if you want to," Smurf said, stripping down to his boxers and getting in the bed.

"It's too late now. I'll call somebody tomorrow," she said stripping down to her sports bra and boy shorts and getting in on the other side of the bed. She thought about it and realized she didn't want to leave. She was kind of feeling young Smurf.

Chapter 9

Omar was in the process of laying some hard dick to Shalika from the back while she ate Zell's pussy, when Zell's water broke all over Shalika's face.

"Oh shit, my water just broke."

"I thought you came," Shalika said.

Omar didn't hear any of the conversation, he was zoned out banging her back out. When he finally nutted and came back to reality, they told him Zell's water broke and he started panicking. They calmed him down long enough for them to all go to the bathroom and get cleaned up. Then Zell called her doctor and they all drove to the hospital in McKinney.

When they got to the hospital, Zell was escorted straight to a room. Omar went with her but came back to the waiting room and sat down with Danielle, Jasmine, Shalika, Kelly, Michelle and Shayla. A little while later Pops and Faye showed up.

"Boy, where is my daughter-in-law?" Faye asked Omar.

"She down there in her room with the doctors. They gonna come get me when the baby comes."

"You get yo' nasty ass up and get down there in that delivery room and see my granddaughter into this world. If you hadn't been doing what you was doing to that girl then we wouldn't be here."

"Mama, you trippin'. I ain't did nothing to Zell."

"Boy, get your ass up and get down there. If you woulda kept yo' thang in your pants and out from between them girls' legs we wouldn't be here. I know Shalika pregnant, too. Look at her face getting fatter. You going in there with her too, so you might as well get some experience with this first one."

Omar got up and went down to Zell's room.

"Mama Faye must have made you come in here?"

"Hell naw," he lied, "I just decided to come and watch my baby girl come into this world."

"Yeah right. Mama Faye out there."

Six hours later, the doctor handed Omar a crying, seven-pound baby girl. She immediately stopped crying when he looked into her hazel green eyes.

"Hey, Omari, daddy got you now. You don't have to cry."

She looked at him for a moment then she pissed all over him.

"Omari, you pee-peed on daddy. You gon' get a spanking," he told her, rocking her in his arms. She looked up at him and smiled and his heart melted. He didn't even know he was crying until the tears started dropping on Omari.

Three days later Zell and Omari were at home. Pops and Faye stayed over until everything was settled with the baby. Faye just really wanted to be there so she could spoil Omari. With so much activity in the house, Omar knew that he wouldn't be able to get any alone time with his daughter, so he called a meeting at the spot.

He took Em with him. When he got to the meeting everyone was already there. "Alright, everybody. Tell me where we at on the work and how much y'all got left."

Glenn was the first one to speak. "We got about two hundred bricks left. Them could be gone in two days, a week or a couple of hours."

"I got about ten pounds left. That shit will be gone by the end of the day."

"I got about ten pounds of the meth left," Dell said.

"The pills are basically over with. I'll be on empty before the day is over with," Dub said.

"What's up with you, Dre?"

"The initial two thousand is gone. We selling what I cut off the two thousand. I put my whip game down and made three outta the two. So, we on some straight profit now."

"Alright. I'ma call my boy and re-up. We should be good in the next couple of days or so. I'll call y'all when we get right." As they all started to leave, Omar called Glenn. "Bro, we might as well start counting this money. You got something to do?"

"Naw, I'm free. Let's go ahead and get this shit done."

"Em, call J-Low and K-Rock and tell them we need them over here and to bring them six money counters in the basement. Tell them to see if Pops wanna come too. We need all the help we can get. I ain't trying to be in this bitch all day and night."

While they were waiting on the money counters and the girls to show up, Omar called Enrique. "What's up, old man? You doing alright?"

"I was just thinking about you. Congratulations. I hear you have a beautiful little baby girl. How is she doing?"

"Thank you. She is doing well. I just can't get any time alone with her right now 'cause my mom and pops, Zell, the other girls, and especially her older sister. So, I'm not getting any time with her right now."

"I know how you feel. I went through that with my daughters. You will have eighteen years to catch up on this time you missed. I have a present coming to little Omari."

"Thanks. I called because—"

"Hey, I'm sure I know why you called, but go to Marie and she has a safe phone that you can call me from in the basement."

"Well, I won't be back home until later. I will call you then."

"Okay son, but check your storage unit. I'll talk to you later," Enrique said before hanging up.

"Damn, this old man never ceases to amaze me. He already knows the baby's name and he's sending her a present. Call Jay and tell him to go by the storage unit and see what's in there. We might already be loaded up. Tell him don't touch shit; just let us know what's in there."

"I'm on it." Glenn said.

A little while later the girls showed up with Pops and they started counting the money. Omar had a walk-in safe built in the basement and each one of them had a designated spot where they put their money.

Pops hooked them up with some of his old school crip homies who were still in the game moving weight. They were being cautious but moving the product at a fast pace. On good days they were pulling in over a million a day. Four hours later they were through counting Dub's money.

"Dub shit straight. The young nigga did his thang." Glenn said.

"Let's count Jay shit next." Omar said.

They went to the basement and came back with the bags for Jay. They went right in and started counting. An hour and a half later Jay was cleared. Next, they started counting Dell bags. Once Dell was cleared, they moved on to Dre's shit and cleared him.

"Man, this nigga Dre a fool with that whip game. I thought you was bad, Glenn, but this nigga Dre might got you," Omar teased.

"Nigga, I'm the baddest nigga in the city. Don't start declaring no top dog until we count my shit."

"Since you talking that shit, let's go ahead and get on top of your shit."

"Let's do this," Glenn said heading to the basement to get his bags.

The whole while they were counting his money, Glenn was talking shit. "See, I was raised by two of the baddest hustlers the city done ever seen. My daddy was a hustler, my mama was a hustler, so it ain't nothing left but for me to be a better hustler. Back in the day they used to call me, 'Get Money Glenn' 'cause I was always known to get the bag."

"Omar, why you get this nigga started?" Pops asked.

"Pops, you know this nigga just talking. His shit looks short anyway," Omar said, enjoying getting Glenn crunk.

"Boy, if my shit short, Popeye a punk, and the whole world knows Popeye was a beast. Youngster, I was doing this shit when you was still in junior high. Who you think you got the game from? You got the game sitting back watching me."

"I wasn't even paying no attention to you, my nigga."

"Boy, stop playing. You know I was your hero growing up."

"Sorry to burst your bubble but Malcolm X and Obama was my heroes growing up," Omar said laughing.

"Nigga, please. I almost forgot while we were out hustling you thought you was Romeo. If it wasn't for me showing you how to get money you'd be married with children."

"The nigga is married with children," Pops said and they all burst out laughing.

"Pops, stay out this and let me handle this nickel rock boy."

"I came in the game moving weight youngster," Glenn said.

When they finally got through counting Gleen's money, Glenn was sitting back in a chair with his feet propped up on the table, smoking a cigar like a real boss. "Give it to me straight," Glenn said, puffing on his cigar.

"Well, big bro, after counting all this money and checking the books on what everybody was supposed to have brought back, I can't even stunt on you. Big bro, you a hustling muthafucka."

"Thank you, thank you." Glenn said, like he was accepting the hustler of the year award. "I wanna thank my mom and dad for blessing me with this hustler's spirit, and my lil' brother for giving me this opportunity. Now, on some serious shit, lil' bro, I want to put something on your brain and I want you to think about it before you make a decision."

"What you talking about, nigga?"

"Bro, I want you to retire from this side of the game and let me run this shit and you just focus on the business side and raising my nieces and taking care of your family. I got this shit."

"I been thinking the same thing. I just didn't know how to bring it to you," Pops said.

Omar sat back and thought for a minute. It would be nice if he didn't have to come to the spot and worry about keeping everything in order. He could sit back, open some more clubs, sports bars and shit like that. He really wanted to open a few strip clubs and get into real estate. He needed to find some kind of way to clean this money up and make it legal. The only reason he was still in the game was because he didn't want to leave his people out in the fields while he sat back like a house nigga. "You got that, big bro. Let's see how this show go. I'ma focus on making this money legal for all of us."

"I got this shit, lil' bro. Now you can focus on the business side and let me handle the dirty work."

Omar took a million dollars and threw it to Em and told her, "Split this with your girls and let's all head to the house."

They loaded the money in the cars and took it to Omar's house and locked it in his walk-in safe, then he went and found Marie. "You have a phone in the basement that I'm supposed to call the old man on?"

"Yes, yes, come. I show you." She took him down to the basement and showed him the phone and dialed the old man.

"Hey, what's happening," Omar said when he answered.

"I have a friend who will come by and meet you. His name is George McGuire and he will pick up the money you have for me. If you have any money that you want to make legal, you give it to him and pay him three million and he will open up a bank account in the Caymans for you and deposit your funds. Untraceable and legal, you will get a bank card that you can use anywhere in the world."

"Is it safe? I can't take any loss right now. My whole team is depending on me."

"Trust me, the guy is a wizard. He is the father of one of your old friends."

"Who?"

"The guy Todd that hangs out with Rudy."

"College boy Todd? The half Asian guy?"

"Yes, the one you speak of."

"Okay."

"I take it you found a little surprise at the storage unit, huh?"

"Yeah, that was right on time. Hey, I wanted to let you know that I'm going to take a backseat and let my brother handle the streets and I'm going to focus on the business side of the operation."

"That is a very wise decision. The head must never get his hands dirty. I take it that you haven't seen the present for little Omari yet, eh? It is there. Check it out and call me later and let me know how you like it."

"Okay and thank you." He ended the call and went upstairs. He looked in on Omari and sitting at the foot of her bed was two four-month-old, fully trained German Shepherds. They had collars on with their names. The boy was King and the girl was Queen. Both dogs got up and came over to Omar and sniffed him then sat at his feet looking up at him. "Hey, King and Queen. Y'all watching over my baby girl?"

The dogs jumped up on him, wagging their tails. He rubbed their heads and told them to sit. They immediately sat down. He went over to the baby's crib and looked in. Omari was laying there staring at him. He picked her up, checked her diaper to see if she was wet and laid down on the floor with her in his arms. King and Queen came over on the side of them.

When Zell got up later that night to go check on Omari, she found all four of them on the floor sleeping soundly.

Chapter 10

Lisa bottled up the rest of the gallons that Robert had and they drove to South Dallas where her little cousins had a spot. They pulled up to a small white house where three young niggas were sitting on the porch.

"Them my cousins right there. All three of they little bad asses. Them niggas getting the bag though. This a million-dollar spot."

"Them lil' niggas look like they some straight gangstas."

"They is and they 'bout that money, too. Come on, let's go holla at them."

They got out the car and walked up on the porch. The first thing Robert noticed was two choppers laying next to them that was unnoticeable to anyone passing by.

"Hey kinfolk." They all said to Lisa.

"Hey, what y'all bad asses up to?"

"Tryna get that bag." They answered.

"This is my boyfriend, Robert. Robert, these are my cousins. That's T-Ray, Ant and Nick." She said pointing to each one.

Robert nodded to each one and they nodded back. Rob wasn't no friendly ass nigga and he wanted to get that understood off the muscle. So, if they messed up that paper, he wanted them to know that he would be coming back to get at their asses. "I got some straight gorilla piss I'm trying to get off and I know you niggas be selling it sometimes but can't always keep enough of it. So, what's up? Y'all wanna work out a deal with us on getting rid of this shit?"

"We ran out that shit two days ago and can't find nobody with some good shit. These niggas be cutting the shit, making it weak as fuck. Is the shit good, and what kinda deal you talking about?"

She reached in her purse and threw them a bottle. "Test that out and see if it's fire."

T-Ray caught the bottle, looked at it and saw how yellow it was and said, "It looks like some straight piss." He pulled out a Newport and dipped the tip of it in the bottle. Then, he sat the bottle on the porch and flipped the Newport upside down and watched it drain down the whole cigarette. When the drain touched the filter, he pulled out his lighter and lit the Newport by barely letting the flame touch it. When it was lit, he took two long pulls on it and passed it to his brother Ant. He took two long pulls and passed it to Nick. Nick passed it to Lisa and Lisa passed it to Rob. The three brothers looked at each other, smiling and nodding.

"That's that click-em-juice right there. We'll fuck with you on that." T-Ray said.

Lisa or Rob didn't hear him. They were locked in a *I wanna fuck the shit outta you* stare, smiling at each other.

"Lisa," T-Ray said a little louder, breaking their trance. "What kinda deal you tryna make? That's that shit right there."

"I got a hundred thousand already bottled up in twenties and fifties. Y'all keep thirty stacks and give me seventy. That's free money right there. Y'all already got the customers but no product. So now you got the product and it's that shit."

"That's a bet kinfolk. We gonna need some more of this in a couple of days."

"I was gon' take some to your uncle in Oak Cliff but I'ma let y'all niggas get the bread. Call me when you get low and I'ma bring you another load of it."

"That's a bet."

Robert went to the trunk and got the bag out with the bottles in it and sat it on the porch next to him.

T-Ray looked inside the bag and sat it back on the porch. "I got you. This shit fire, we might be through with this shit tomorrow. Look at them niggas," he said pointing to his two brothers who were slumped.

"Ain't nobody slumped, nigga. I'm just resting my eyes. I'm fully alert. I know you, big homie." He said to Robert without raising his head. "You big Robert from the Nawf."

"Yeah, that's me." Robert said easing his hand toward his waist in case the nigga said something slick.

"Forest Lane, that's our block. Get to bullshittin' we'll knock you out yo' socks," Ant started singing.

"That's my shit, right there." Robert said smiling.

"Bro, you put the whole Nawf on with that bitch. I flow, too, me and Nick. We got a whole studio in the house. Come fuck with us and let's put together a mix tape or a banger for the streets."

"You nice?" Robert asked.

Without even answering Ant started flowing and Nick woke up and hopped on the flow. Robert stood there nodding, listening, then he jumped on the flow with a nasty ass freestyle.

"Damn, my nigga, y'all niggas sound good together. That shit was dope and that was just some off the top of the head shit. Imagine what y'all niggas would sound like if y'all had worked on that shit." T-Ray said.

"I wanna fuck with you, Big Rob. Come through and fuck with us."

"That shit was dope, my nigga. I'ma come through and fuck with y'all fo' sho'." When they got back in the car, Robert said, "Find us a motel. That dip got my dick harder than a muthafucka. I'm finna fuck the shit out of you."

"That shit got my pussy soaking wet, too." Lisa said, grabbing his hand and putting it inside her panties.

"Damn." He said pulling his hand out soaked with her juices. He licked all of her juices off his fingers.

"Oh shit, I just nutted, watching you do that. You nasty, but I like that freaky shit."

"You taste like strawberry ice cream." He said sticking his finger back in her panties and licking her juices off his fingers again.

"Fuck that motel, I'm finna pull over somewhere so you can eat this pussy."

"You ain't said shit."

A few minutes later Lisa parked in a good store parking lot and slid the seat all the way back. She pulled one leg out of her pants and panties, leaned back against the door with her legs wide open and told Robert, "There it is. You was talking that gangsta shit. Is you 'bout it?"

He didn't even respond. He just dove in and started eating her pussy like a starving Ethiopian.

"Damn, nigga, you sucking the shit outta this pussy," Lisa told him, lifting her ass off the seat while grinding her pussy on his face.

He sucked her to three nuts right there in the store parking lot and then he licked her pussy clean, savoring every drop of her juices.

When she was finally able to get dressed, she told him, "You went FED today. Now, pull that dick out. I'ma go just as hard as you did."

"Let's find that room. I'm tryna get up in that pussy."

"You definitely gonna hit this pussy. But, I'm finna suck that dick right now," she said reaching to unzip his pants. She got his pants down and started deep throating his dick. She cupped his balls in one hand and gave him some slow throat.

He did as he was told but he was being too gentle. Lisa wanted to be manhandled.

"Nigga, fuck my throat like you be hitting this pussy. Ain't gon' be no gagging and shit, nigga. I'ma beast for real.

Now, fuck my face like you tryna bust the last nut of your life."

Rob grabbed the back of her head and started slamming dick down her throat. Lisa was moaning and slamming her face in his crotch, meeting every thrust. He couldn't last. He shot a load of cum down her throat and she swallowed every drop. Then she licked his dick clean like a popsicle. She kissed the head before she put it back in his pants and zipped him up.

"That shit was good?" She asked.

"Hell yeah!"

"Now we can go get that room so you can get in this pussy."

Chapter 11

Smurf woke up in the middle of the night and felt Trina's soft ass against his hard dick. He tried moving back a little, but she scooted right back up against him. He finally said fuck it and wrapped his arms around her and went back to sleep.

The next morning, when they woke up, he took a shower and found her a new toothbrush. While she was handling her business in the bathroom, he told her he was going to walk up the street to his mama's house and get the keys of Riff Raff's car and he would be right back.

He put his pistol in his waist and left. He hit a few alleys when he could so he wouldn't be seen by anyone and finally made it to the house behind his mom's. He sat in the backyard for a while just watching the house. When he was sure the law wasn't watching, he climbed over the gate and unlocked the back door with his key.

It seemed strange, the house being empty and quiet. He couldn't remember Red Tina's house ever being empty or quiet. He thought about the fact that she was gone and that he would never hear her voice again or never get to hug her again and a wave of sadness swept over him.

He went to her bedroom and sat on her bed for a long moment. Finally, he got up and went to his old bedroom and pushed the dresser out of the way and moved a corner of the carpet back. He lifted the floorboard and pulled out a black bag that his brother Riff Raff hid in his room. He told Smurf that this was emergency money. It was sixty-five thousand in the bag.

Smurf found his old school backpack and put the money in it. He went back to the floor and got two brand new Draco's with hundred-round clips and a bullet proof vest. He added several boxes of bullets and closed the spot up, put the carpet back in place and pushed the dresser back to its normal spot.

He got the spare set of keys to Riff Raff's Yukon that he kept parked down the street in old lady Mrs. Johnson's driveway and started to leave. He finally noticed all the dried blood and bullet holes in the walls when he walked back out into the hallway and living room.

That wave of sadness tried to take over him again, but he pushed it away and walked right out the back door with the backpack on his back. He went back down the alley until he got to Mrs. Johnson's house and climbed over the gate. He looked at the house and saw Mrs. Johnson looking at him from the kitchen window. She waved at him and he waved back. He went to the back door and said, "I'm taking the truck, Mrs. Johnson."

"How you holding up? You alright?"

"Yes, ma'am, I'm alright."

"Well, I can tell you in a hurry. You be careful and stop by and see me when you can."

"I will, Mrs. Johnson."

Smurf went to the driveway and got in the truck and drove back down to the house where he left Trina. He got out the truck and went back in the house wondering if Trina had left or not. When he walked in the bedroom, she was sitting in the middle of the bed watching TV.

She smiled at him as he came in the room. "I'm hungry," she said.

"Me too. What you want to eat?"

"IHOP."

"I was thinking the same thing. It's one right down the street. Let's go tear that bitch up."

"Let's go."

He locked the house up and they got in the truck and drove down to the IHOP. While they were waiting on the food Smurf asked Trina, "You plan on staying with me forever?"

"I don't know. You want me to stay with you forever?"

"You cool people and I'm enjoying your company, so you can stay as long as you want."

"Why you didn't take advantage of that opportunity last night? I know you wanted to. I felt you was ready."

"Didn't want to seem too anxious. I really got too much on my mind to start thinking about something else. Plus, I didn't want to approach you like some jump off."

"I thought you didn't like me or something."

"Naw, that ain't the case. I just got a lot on my mind."

"I gotta go to work tonight. You gonna take me and pick me up?"

"Yeah, where you work at?"

"I work at that 7-Eleven right across from that hotel, the Comforter Suites off 35 in Carrollton."

"Let's head out that way right now. I'ma get a room at that hotel for a few weeks. You cool with chillin' there?"

"Yeah, that's cool. I work right across the street so I can walk back to the room. I need some of my clothes and stuff from the house. I'ma see if—"

"Once we get the room you can take the truck and go get the stuff you need. I'll chill here until you get back."

"Alright."

After they ate, they drove out to the hotel and Trina went in and got the room for a month with her identification and the money he gave her.

She came back out a few minutes later and gave him an envelope with two keycards and the room number. He drove to the side entrance and parked, and they went in and found the room.

As they were unlocking the door to their room a black couple came up the hallway and went into the room next door to them. They both spoke before they went in and closed the door.

"That nigga looked kinda familiar," Smurf told Trina.

"He did, didn't he?"

They went in the room and closed the door. Smurf looked around and saw that it was like a one-bedroom apartment. It had a bedroom, a living room and a kitchen area with a stove and refrigerator.

"This is kinda nice," Trina said.

"Yeah, it is. Here, you might as well go and get your clothes and things." He said, handing her the keys to the truck. "Hold up. You can drive can't you?" He asked, smiling.

"Yeah, boy, I can drive. I been had my license since I was sixteen. I got a little Mustang. It's just in the shop. Some old ass white lady ran into my shit a few weeks ago and the insurance people tried to give me a Malibu, but they wanted me to pay twenty-five dollars a day to use it. I said bullshit, I'll use the bus until my shit get fixed, then I'm changing my insurance over to Geico or something."

"Them insurance people want they bread," he said turning on the TV and laying across the bed.

"Well, I'll be back in a few," she said heading for the door.

"Here," he said, giving her one of the key cards.

After she left, Smurf called Omar.

"What's up, you good?"

"Yeah, I'm over here at the Comforter Suites off I-35 in Carrollton."

"What you doing out there?"

"Come through and holla at me."

"I'm on my way."

Chapter 12

About an hour later Omar pulled up at the hotel with K-Rock, J-Low, and Em. As they were approaching Smurf's room the door to the room next to them opened and Lisa stepped out on her way to the ice machine.

"Lisa, what you doing way out here?" Omar asked.

"Hey, Short Dogg. I'm out here with your boy Robert."

"What Robert?"

"Mob Rob."

"Stop playing. When my nigga get back in town?"

"He been here about a month."

"Go get the nigga and tell him I'm next door. I gotta check on my lil' nigga. Y'all come fuck with us."

She went back in the room and they all knocked on the door and went in the room with Smurf.

"What up, Smurf? Tell me something good," Omar said. They stepped into the bedroom and Smurf told Omar everything that he had found out about Yogi and Pam. Omar couldn't believe it. "Lil bro, you sure? That don't sound like Yogi."

"I wouldn't have believed it either, but her homegirl called her on the phone and let me listen. They somewhere in the country right now laid up. I heard the nigga voice in the background."

"That nigga really outta line for that. He could have told a nigga what was going on."

"That's what I'm saying. All this shit was him and D-Man trippin' over Pam. My mama and my brother gone 'cause this nigga a tender dick."

"That nigga D-Man a real live pussy nigga. I shoulda murked his bitch ass a long time ago."

"He gonna get his. Him and every one of them niggas that was with him. I'm not going to rest until everyone of them niggas ain't breathing. I'm thinking about sending Yogi weak ass with them."

"I don't know what to say about that. You need to think long and hard about that before you make any moves on that."

"Yeah, I feel you."

They went back in the front room when they heard a knock on the door. Omar went to the door and opened it; Robert was standing there smiling with Lisa on the side of him. "My nigga," Omar said grabbing Rob in a bear hug. "How long you been back in the city?"

"I been back a little over a month."

"Man, why you ain't holla at me?"

"I been trying to get back on my feet. I came back with some gallons of wet. Me and baby been getting off them," he said pointing to Lisa.

"I coulda hooked you up with some more shit. So, you ain't seen nobody since you been back?"

"Naw, I just been chillin' with Lisa."

"Let me call Dub, D-Money, and Bobi," Omar said, pulling out his phone. "You heard about all the shit that's done went down since you been gone?"

"Yeah, I been hearing bits and pieces but put me up on the real. What the fuck got into them niggas?"

"Come to find out Kim was behind all the shit. But the nigga Mack made a deal with the laws to get out of jail on a pistol charge. The FEDs picked the charge up. So, when I found out about it I called a meeting and put the shit in front of everybody. Kim, Murda, and Mack tried to make it like wasn't shit wrong with what the nigga was doing."

"What kinda deal the nigga make with twelve?"

"My nigga, this shit crazy. I bonded the nigga out, so I guess they got my number off his bond papers. A homicide detective called me and straight up told me that he took the federal hold off Mack in exchange for him finding some witnesses to testify on the New Orleans nigga that killed Kels."

"That nigga foul for that and Kim know he was," Rob said.

"My nigga, she admitted that she set the whole play up. It was her idea to do that so Mack could get out of jail. Fred told them niggas that they were foul so some kinda way they got Fred to meet up with them. They tried to get him to go along with they little plot to murk me. When he told them he wasn't with that bullshit, they smoked him."

"That was some foul ass shit them niggas was on," Robert said, shaking his head.

"Ain't nobody got no weed in this muthafucka?" Omar asked.

"I got some smoke and a bottle of Patron. Lisa, can you go get some of that weed and a bottle of Patron?"

Before she could get to the door it opened and Trina was standing there with three bags of clothes.

Smurf went to the door and helped her with the bags before introducing her. "This my friend Trina."

"Trina, look at you girl, looking all grown. Where yo' crazy brother?" Omar asked.

"Hey, what's up Short Dogg? I am grown; I'm nineteen now." She said smiling. "I just saw Mark. he alright."

They sat around talking, drinking, smoking, and catching up with Robert. B-Dub, D-Money, and Bobi all came through. Everyone was happy to see Robert back in town.

Omar pulled Robert to the side later on and told him the rundown on Smurf and asked him to kind of keep an eye on him for him. He gave Smurf a hundred thousand dollars that Em brought with them so he could have some cash to spend if needed. He also told him that they were going to have a wake for Red Tina this coming week. She didn't want a funeral, so they were going to have the wake and a burial.

Red Tina had told Faye a long time ago, "Bitch, when I die don't let them take me in no church. I don't want no preacher lying over my body telling the church how loving and wonderful I was, knowing he telling a damn lie."

After they all left, Smurf and Trina took a nap. A few hours later they woke up and Trina got ready to go to work. After she left for work, Smurf called his boy, Yaki.

"What's good?"

"What the fuck, my nigga? I been trying to call you for the last few days. What you been up to? I'm ready to ride on these fuck niggas."

"Be patient. We gon' turn them niggas' lights off in due time. I'm tryna bury my mama and my brother first. Where you at? I need to come holla at you about some shit."

"I'm in the hood on the block. Come through and fuck with me."

"I'll be through in a minute."

"Alright, one."

"One."

Smurf got dressed, grabbed his Drako and drove to Oak Cliff. When he pulled up, he saw Yaki and a few of the homies sitting on the porch of the house across the street from his mom's house. He honked the horn and Yaki came over and got in and he pulled off.

"What it do, cuz?" Yaki asked.

"My nigga, I'm finna tell you some shit that don't go nowhere. This shit 'bout to fuck you up."

"That's law, my nigga. What the deal is?"

"Trina been with me the whole time since that night we took her. She put me up on game, why all this shit been happening. That nigga Dee-Man and them young niggas he run with the ones who shot the block up and killed my mama and Yogi."

"Let's get at them niggas tonight. I know where that nigga Crazy, Cuz-Loc, and C-Baby be at. Them niggas stay on Dee-Man dick. So they had to have something to do with it too." Yaki said.

"Listen my nigga, this is the part that's gon' fuck you up. The reason they did the shit ain't got nothing to do with the beef between our hood and theirs. They did the shit 'cause Dee-Man and Yogi beefing over fine ass Pam. She left that nigga Dee-Man and now she fucking with Yogi. The nigga been sneaking off with the bitch."

"Is you sure about that? I just can't see the big homie doing the game like that."

"I'm sure, my nigga. Trina called Pam while I was listening and they were together. The nigga in love with the bitch."

"So basically Yogi got Red Tina, Riff and everybody else killed 'cause he fucking with Pam and him and Dee-Man tripping over her. Why that nigga didn't let us know what the play was so we could be on point?"

"That's what I'm saying."

"That's some foul shit. That bitch must got that snapper to have the OG tripping and slipping like that."

"I know that nigga fucked up. I haven't talked to the nigga since the hospital. I really wanna smoke that nigga too. My mama and brother gone because he tender dicking. I wouldn't even be mad if he had told us beforehand. He knew he was fucking that nigga hoe and he knew Dee-Man was gonna trip about the shit. He coulda told us so we would know what the fuck was going on."

"Yeah, he dead wrong for that."

"I done got mad thinking about this shit all over again. You say you know where them fuck niggas hang out at. Let's ride by that bitch and knock them niggas' heads off."

"Let's go back on the block. I got a hot shot we can use. I know you don't want to do the shit in Riff truck and I need to grab my Drako."

Smurf drove back to the block and parked the truck in Mrs. Johnson' driveway. Yaki got his Drako off the porch and they got in a stolen silver Camaro and drove off.

"Them niggas be hustling in that vacant lot where that old big ass church that burned down a few years ago was."

"Right up the street from them Mexican's car lot?"

"Yeah, that's where they be."

"Go down that next street and park so we can come up the alley and sneak up on them niggas."

"That's what I was gon' do. I'ma smoke everything in sight once I start shooting."

"That's understood. That's what they did to us. Any innocent bystanders are casualties of war. This hood justice." Smurf said.

"And you know this. man."

Yaki parked on the next street in front of a vacant house. They got out and went through the yard to the backyard, climbed over the gate and walked down the alley until they got to the house. They hopped over the fence and went through the yard. When they got to the house they split up. Smurf went to the right and Yaki took the other side.

Smurf got to the front and peeked around the corner of the house and saw four niggas sitting on the porch passing a blunt. He waited a minute to let Yaki get in position before stepping around the house and opening up with the Drako.

He was like ten feet away when he opened up and his first volley of shots hit all four of them. Seconds after he started firing, Yaki opened up. It sounded like a war was going on, but it was only Smurf and Yaki shooting until somebody started firing shots from a pistol about two houses over on Yaki's side of the house. Yaki turned and started letting off shots at whoever was shooting. Then they both unloaded on the whole block, emptying their clips.

Smurf took off running back to the car while switching his clip out with a fresh one. He met up with Yaki in the backyard and they hopped over the gate and made their way back to the car. They got in the car and Yaki slowly drove away. When he got to the end of the block, he turned on the headlights and headed back to the hood.

"Call them niggas on the block and tell them to be on point just in case them fuck niggas try to come through and hit us up." Smurf told Yaki.

Yaki pulled out his phone and called the block and told them to be on point. "Bro, we wet them niggas' asses up. That one nigga started pop locking when them bullets from that Drako started hitting his ass. You seen that?"

"That nigga C-Baby a bitch. He tried to run off and leave them niggas. Always talking that big boy shit, now Riff can get at the hoe nigga when he get wherever a nigga go when this shit is over with. Fuck them niggas. This just the start. Wait til' I really get crunk. I'm gunning at they whole hood if anybody try and help them niggas."

"Nigga, Red Tina helped raise all them hoe ass niggas before we started beefing. and to think them niggas would come shoot up my mama shit. I'ma hurt this nigga Dee-Man real bad. Every chance I get to fuck over something he love, I'ma smoke it and save his bitch ass for last."

"I feel you, my nigga, and I'm all the way down with you til' it's over or I'm dead. Red Tina was like my mama, too. Shit, she was my mama, too. She did more for me than my own mama did." Yaki said before continuing. "You remember that time she caught us skipping school and called us out in the backyard and made us throw them hands with her."

"You remember that shit, nigga?" Smurf asked, smiling.

"Hell yeah, I remember. That's the last fight I lost. She talking about, 'Y'all lil' niggas done got some pussy and been 'round here fucking these lil' bitches so y'all thank y'all grown. Y'all go to school when y'all want to, huh? Well, that's cool, but come on out here to the backyard, and if y'all beat my ass you can do what you wanna do. We just gon' go a couple of rounds with the hands. Word around the hood is that you got something with the fist, Yaki. I got something, too.'" Red Tina said while putting on an old pair of J's.

"Mama, chill out. We ain't trying to go there with you." Smurf said back then.

"Yeah, you gotta be 'cause you ain't in school and you left here going to school. So, we just gon' get a little understanding about who run shit around here. Y'all come on." She said heading to the backyard.

Red Tina was tall and light complected with wide hips, huge breasts and an ass like a buffalo. Her mama was half-Mexican so she had that good black hair like she was Indian.

As soon as they got in the backyard she turned and fired off on Smurf, catching him with a left to the chin that knocked him off his feet. "I'ma get at you in a minute, Yaki, as soon as I dust his ass off. Y'all lil' niggas gon' learn some respect."

Smurf got to his feet mad as a muthafucka. He threw his hands up and started for his mama. He threw a two piece at her that she weaved and caught him with a right to the stomach and another left to the chin that put him back on the ground.

Seeing that Smurf was out of the fight, she turned and shot a combination at Yaki. He easily weaved her punches and said, "Come on, mama Tina, before you get hurt out here."

"I tell you what I'ma do. If you whip me, I'ma give you some of this good ass pussy and I'ma suck yo' dick."

Yaki dick got hard as soon as she said it. He looked at all that ass hanging out the back of her shorts and that fat ass pussy print and said to himself, 'That nigga Smurf just gon' have to be mad at me. I'm finna get me some of that pussy.' "Mama Tina, you tripping."

"Naw, I'm dead ass serious. You win, you get some head and pussy."

Yaki shot a dummy jab at her to see if she would fall for it so he could hit her with a right hand haymaker and put her lights out. Just like he thought, she bit on the dummy. When he threw the haymaker instead of Red Tina trying to get away from it, she stepped into it. His whole fist missed her, and his forearm caught her which did no damage.

Red Tina was right in his grill and she hit him with a four piece combination of six inch punches to the chin. Left, right, left, right. He stumbled and went to the ground dizzy as fuck.

Yaki wanted some of Red Tina's pussy so bad that he lost all thought and jumped right up and ran into two haymakers that put him out cold. When he woke up, he was in Smurf's room laying in the bed with an ice pack across his face. The next day, he and Smurf was at school.

"My nigga, Red Tina had them hands," Yaki said as he pulled back up on the block.

"Let's duck off and see if them fuck niggas gon' come through."

They saw that the block was still jumping. Fiends were coming through and niggas were serving them but everybody was ducked off on a porch, behind a car or something. Nobody was standing out in the open.

After a couple of hours of sitting and waiting, Smurf finally got up and went back to the room. "I'll catch up with you after they bury my mama."

"I'll be there when they bury her, too."

"Alright, call me if something jump off over here."

"I got you."

He got in the truck and drove back to the hotel.

Chapter 13

Smurf went to the wake with Omar and his family. He hadn't seen Shayla in over a week. She was happy to see her big brother and was telling him everything that had happened since he had been gone.

"We got two puppies, King and Queen. They are so pretty, and they are trained to sit and they don't even bark or bite me."

"I want you to come home, Smurf, so you can see the puppies and play with them. Then we can play the Xbox like we used to."

"I'll be home soon, and we'll play with the puppies, and I'll kick your butt on the Xbox."

She started laughing. "I always beat you."

"'Cause you be cheating all the time."

"No, I don't."

"Yes, you do." He said pulling her over in his lap and tickling her. "You do be cheating."

"Uh-uhh, I don't be cheating." She said laughing.

"I love you, lil' sis."

"I love you, too, big brother. You not going to get in trouble, are you?" She asked, looking him in the eyes.

"Naw, I ain't gon' get in no trouble."

They had the wake at Golden Gate Funeral home. It was hundreds of people there. Smurf saw Yogi but he stayed on the other side of the room from him.

Red Tina had a brother that was doing life in prison but some kind of way he was allowed to attend the wake in handcuffs and shackles surrounded by three armed prison guards.

"What's up Uncle Skip?" Smurf said, recognizing him as he came through the door.

"Is that you Lil' Robert? Damn lil' nigga you looking grown. How old you is?"

"I'll be sixteen in two weeks."

"You is grown. What's been going on? What happened to my sister?"

"It's a long story and I know you don't want me to tell you the real deal in front of these Po Pos."

"Naw, that wouldn't be a good idea."

"I'ma write you or maybe I'll get somebody to bring me to visit you." He looked around and saw Em and called her over." Em, this is my Uncle Skip."

"How you doing? I'm Em."

"I need to go visit him and let him know the real with my mama and his sister. Will you take me?"

"Sure, when you want to go?"

"In the next week or so."

"Just let me know when and I'll take you."

"Hey, let me get your info so I can add you to my visiting list. I need your name, age, and address."

She went and found a pen and paper and wrote the information down and gave it to the officers to give to him. A few minutes later, three sheriff deputies walked in with Tiger, Smurf's father, handcuffed and shackled.

"What's up, Pops?" Smurf said, hugging his dad.

"What y'all niggas got going on out here? You know the streets talk."

As he was talking, Yogi walked over and hugged his dad and spoke.

"What's up, dad?"

"You niggas is what's up. How you niggas get caught slippin' like this?"

Yogi started to speak but looked over at the deputies.

"I need a few minutes to talk to my boys," Tiger said to the officers.

"Let's sit you down over here and y'all can talk," one of the deputies said pointing to some chairs. They walked over and sat down and the deputies stepped a few feet away so they could have some privacy.

"Now what the fuck is going on out here?" Tiger asked.

"You know we beefing with them Glendale niggas and they caught us slipping and shot the house and the block up."

Before Tiger could say anything, Smurf said, "So that's what happened?"

"What you mean lil' nigga? What you know that I don't know?"

"I don't know shit you don't know. But I know some shit you ain't telling us."

"What you know nigga?" Yogi asked.

"I know this shit ain't had nothing to do with our beef with them niggas. I know you fucking Dee-Man girl and you and that nigga beefing over that bitch Pam. That's why my mama and brother is laying up there in caskets. You forgot to tell us that part of the story."

"Nigga, who is you to tell me who I can fuck?"

"This nigga foul, daddy. He knew he was beefing with that nigga Dee-Man over Pam. but, the nigga didn't tell us shit, so we got caught slippin' and my mama and big brother is dead because of him. The least he could have did was told us what was going on so we could be on point but naw, this nigga was only thinking about his self and his dick."

When Smurf finally finished going in on Yogi, Tiger said, "What's up with this shit here, Yogi? I know Smurf ain't sitting here lying about this shit."

"I didn't know that nigga was going to do that shit."

"But you been fucking the nigga bitch and y'all been beefing over the hoe so you had to know that something might go down. You didn't think to alert the homies or your own brother?"

"I thought the shit would blow over. I never thought that nigga would go this low over some pussy."

"That's why I always told you niggas to stop thoughting and start thinking. That was some rookie shit you did and we all paying the consequences for it. My wife and my son gone cause of your mistake. Nigga, you better get this shit right before I touched the streets. I didn't raise no pussies, cuz. You wanna play house with that girl. Nigga what the fuck you hiding for? That's what we do, take niggas bitches. I took yo' mama from a bitch ass nigga. I give a fuck what hood she from. Yo' mama a Blood, I'ma full blue Crip. You fucked up not telling the hood. I already knew the whole story. I just wanted to see if you was gonna tell me. I know you been shacked up with the girl at that house on the lake in Rockwall since it happened. I want every nigga ass who fired a shot. Don't make me hate you nigga. Get that shit took care of and soon. Tiger stood up and told the deputies. "Let me sit over here with my brother in law," he told them nodding towards where Skip was sitting."

Yogi walked off and sat down at the front of the room. Smurf kinda felt bad for him until he looked to the front of the room and saw the two caskets with his mother and brother's bodies inside them.

A few minutes later, Smurf saw Trina and Pam come in the room together. Tiger called Pam over and started talking to her while Trina came over and spoke to him.

"How you doing?" She asked.

"I'm good. We gotta sit down and have a talk tonight."

"About what?"

"About us and what we are doing. It's all good, I just want us to be on the same page."

"Alright."

He saw Pam leave from talking to Tiger and go sit next to Yogi. She kissed him and they started talking. Smurf looked over at his father and his father nodded at him. Smurf looked at Trina and told her, "I want you to stay by my side. We ain't hiding from nobody." He grabbed her hand and together they went and took their seats next to Yogi and Pam.

Smurf looked around and saw Omar and his family and a lot of people he hadn't seen in a while. Finally, they opened the casket's and everyone went by and paid their last respects and it was over.

Smurf was ready for war.

Chapter 14

Yogi left the wake for his mother and brother with murder on his mind. He knew his father was disappointed in him and after he sat back and replayed the whole situation over in his mind. He was disappointed in his self.

He should have told the homies what was going on with Pam and Dee-Man instead of sneaking around and trying to keep their relationship on the low. He couldn't even come up with a good excuse of why he was hiding their relationship.

At first, he was just fucking Pam. But after a while, he started seeing how real she was and he started falling more and more for her. Not to mention that she was one of the baddest bitches to ever walk the streets of Oak Cliff. Plus, she was a stone cold freak in the bedroom.

Pam was about five foot three and weighed a hundred and fifty four pounds. Her face kinda reminded you of the singer Saweetie. Pam had ass, titties and thighs for days. Yogi loved the way everything she wore gripped her ass like some stockings. She was from the hood but she was far from a hoe. Dee-Man was her first boyfriend and had popped her cherry when she was still in high school. They had been together for seven years until Yogi came along and took her away from the nigga Dee-Man.

One night, Pam and Trina went to the club after she had got into a big argument with Dee-Man over having a hickey on his neck that she didn't put there. He kept lying telling her that it was a rash on his neck but Pam wasn't trying to hear that.

Yogi saw them at the club and sent Pam a bottle of champagne to her table. They talked and danced the whole night. Yogi got her number and started hitting her up on the phone. They talked for hours and hours every chance they got. Finally, Yogi rented a suite for the weekend and they went to the casino in Lake Charles and spent the weekend gambling.

Pam won ten thousand dollars playing Blackjack. She was drinking shots of Tequila and feeling good. When they got back to the room, Yogi sucked her pussy for an hour straight, then he pounded her back out for the rest of the night.

After that weekend, they started sneaking off every chance they got until Dee-Man got hip and followed her to a party Yogi was having. She finally admitted that she was fucking Yogi and told him that she didn't want to see him again.

A few nights later, Dee-Man saw Yogi at the club and started talking shit. They almost came to punches before club security intervened and broke it up. A few nights later, Dee-Man and his boys came through and shot the block up. Since then, they had been going back and forth until they came through and caught them slipping and killed Riff Raff, Red Tina, and several more people.

Yogi knew he had to put in some work before his father came home. Tiger loved his boys but he didn't tolerate any weak shit from his kids. If you had to put in some work, Tiger expected his boys to handle their business. Fuck the consequences.

Pam was lying next to Yogi sleeping. She was naked and laying on her stomach. He looked at her ass and started getting aroused. He rolled over on her and eased his dick inside of her always wet pussy.

"Uhm," she moaned, opening her legs wider, giving him full access to her pussy.

He started out slow stroking her but the warm tightness of her had him in a zone and pounding away in her in no time.

"Damn, this pussy good."

"Nut in this pussy, baby," she urged him on, rotating her hips to meet his every thrust.

"I'm finna nut in this pussy," he said getting more turned on by the sounds her pussy was making.

"I'm cumming on that dick daddy. Oh shit, I'm cumming."

Feeling her pussy tighten up and grip his dick, he lost it and started pounding her back out and before long, he was nutting in her pussy.

He rolled off her, breathing hard. When she finally went back to sleep, Yogi got up and went to the basement where he got out his bulletproof vest, his twin nine millimeters, an Uzi and his beloved pistol grip shotgun. He dressed up in all black and went outside and got in his old Camry.

***

Lil Gutta was straight outta Glendale. He was one of Dee-Man's main lil' niggas. He was riding in the first car that came through firing shots at Red Tina's house. He didn't have anything against Riff Raff, Red Tina or Yogi, he was just shooting cause he wanted to be down. He had put in a lot of work for Dee-Man, shooting niggas in the back, in the dark and all kinds of other little coward shit just to get a name in the hood. He wanted to be known for being tough or ready to put in work. But really, he was a straight bitch.

He laid in the bed sound asleep while his baby mama and lil' girl was tied up, gagged and placed in another room. The intruder came back in the room where Lil' Gutta was at and slapped the shit out of him with his gun.

Lil Gutta tried to jump up after being slapped awake but he found that he was tied to the bed and couldn't move.

"What the fuck? Where my daughter and my girl at?" He asked the masked gunman.

The gunman slapped him again. "Shut the fuck up, I'm asking the questions around here."

Lil Gutta remained quiet and watched as the gunman peeled his mask off and there stood Yogi with an evil smile on his face. Lil' Gutta pissed all over his self and immediately started talking.

"Yogi, Dee-Man ordered the hit on yo' mama house. I wasn't nowhere around when the shit went down," he lied.

Yogi slapped the shit out of him again. "Nigga stop lying to me. Nigga, I been fucking yo' baby mama since high school. She already told me the real. So save that punk shit for somebody that wants to hear it."

Being the bitch nigga he was he couldn't do nothing but think to himself, *'Damn, Stacy been giving this nigga my pussy.'*

"Where Dee-Man at?"

"The last I heard a couple of days ago, he was laying low at Jo-Jo spot. Him and Jo-Jo been fucking around since you started fucking with Pam."

"Since you being so honest and shit I'ma let yo' baby mama and yo' lil' girl live."

"Please don't kill me, Yogi. I ain't have shit to do with that shit Dee-Man pulled," Lil' Gutta begged with tears running down his face.

Yogi didn't even pay any attention to his pleas for sympathy. He just upped his nine millimeter with the silencer on it and let five of them off in Gutta's face. Then, he left out the front door.

Yogi drove by Jo-Jo spot to see if he ran across Dee-Man but nobody was home. He drove back to Oak Cliff and went by a few spots that Dee-Man hung out at but the block was empty.

Finally, he went by Dee-Man's mama house. The house was dark and quiet. Two cars were parked in the driveway. Yogi got his Uzi with the hundred round clip and lit the house up the same way Dee-Man shot his mama house up.

Then he drove home, parked his car in the garage, put his guns in the stash spot and went upstairs and climbed in the bed with Pam.

Chapter 15

Lil Smurf was fucking the cowboy shit outta Trina. Her legs were on his shoulders and he had her pent up against the headboard, pounding in and out of her pussy. It had been months since she had some dick and Smurf was giving her all the dick she had missed and more.

Whatever Big Tiger had talked to them about, it made Yogi and Smurf get on their shit. When they finally got back to the room from the wake, he rolled a fat ass blunt and took a couple of pulls from the bottle that Robert and Omar left the other day.

"You really wanna fuck with me?" He asked, sitting on the couch in his boxers firing the blunt up.

"You already know I do so why you asking me something you already know the answer to?"

"I'm just trying to get this shit understood and laid out right in front of us. Cause, ain't no turning back once we get started. You already know we beefing with yo' hood and I'm not gon' stop until that nigga Dee-Man is dead and all the niggas that was with him who fired a shot at my mama house too. I need to know that you down with me through whatever."

"I'm down with you until the end. But, I ain't gon' be no bitch that you can cheat on and treat like dirt. If you gon' be my man then you gonna have to treat me like yo' queen and respect me."

"I ain't no fuck nigga, so that goes without saying. Don't give my pussy away to no nigga. I don't care if I'm locked up or what. Once we lock this shit in, ain't no going back."

"That's the same way I feel. But how you gon' claim this pussy when you ain't even put yo' name on it yet?"

"I'm about to handle that right now. But, I need you to call Mark and let him know what the business is. You might as well let me talk to him."

She went and got her cellphone and called her brother. "Hey bro, what you doing?"

She listened for a minute before she said, "I just wanted to call you and let you know that me and Smurf locked in. He my man now and I hope you give us your blessings."

Smurf motioned for her to put the phone on speaker so he could hear his response.

"I ain't trippin' bout that shit as long as that nigga don't fuck over you and treat you right. If you feel like he the nigga for you, then do you."

"Yo' sister ain't no dummy. He gon' do right."

"Well then that shit settled. Tell that lil' nigga the set done kicked that nigga Dee-Man out. So whatever they got going with him, the hood ain't involved. That shit he pulled we didn't know shit about. It's too many people getting killed and shot over some shit they ain't had nothing to do with and them niggas beefing over Pam. Both of them niggas weak to be fighting over some pussy. It's too much pussy out here to be fighting over one."

"Boy you crazy. I'ma call you later."

"Alright bye."

She put the phone on the table and told Smurf. "You heard what he said so ain't no more excuses."

"Come on over here so I can make this shit official," he said taking a handful of condoms from his pants pocket that was laying across the couch.

"What you finna do with them?" She asked pointing at the condoms.

"I'm finna fuck the shit outta you."

"I don't do the plastic. I gotta have that raw dick to cum," she told Smurf, taking her shirt and pants off.

"Since you my girl now, you can get this raw dick," he said looking at her standing in her thong and matching bra.

Trina was dark complected and looked like Kelly Rowland. She was only about four foot eleven, but she was slim fine. She had a nice ass and breasts. The front of her thong looked like she had a boxing glove stuffed in it.

They laid on the couch tongue kissing for a long time while he caressed her body. He started nibbling on her neck and kissing her shoulders. He took her bra off and licked and sucked her titties for twenty minutes before he moved down to her stomach. He could tell she was getting turned on because she couldn't be still.

He took her thong off and opened her legs. He just stared at her pussy for a long time, before he started licking her thighs. Finally, he opened her pussy lips and saw her clit staring back at him. He licked it a couple of times before he started sucking on it while moving his tongue around it in a circular motion.

"Oh shit Smurf, just like that. That shit feels so good," she said, grabbing the back of his head.

Smurf had never ate pussy before. He had watched a million porno movies and got his head game from watching niggas eat pussy on the movies. He knew he had to step his game up fucking with Trina. She wasn't no little girl. She was a grown woman so he knew he had to put it down.

He nibbled, sucked, licked and kissed on her pussy for almost an hour. She busted three nuts on his face. When she finally pulled him up, he had pussy juice all in his eyebrows. She kissed him, sucking on his tongue, tasting her juices on his tongue.

She pulled his boxers off and said, "Damn boy, all that dick."

She rubbed his dick all over her face before she took the head in her mouth. Trina was a freak but she was the kind of freak that only let it out when she had a man. She was feeling Smurf and he was young. She felt like she could put her sex game on him and lock the nigga in forever.

She sucked on the head a couple of times, then started giving him the best head he'd ever had in his life. She gripped his thighs and gave him some slow head, going all the way down and all the way up making sure she hit the head every time she came up. It didn't take Smurf long before he was shooting a bucket load of nut down her throat.

"Was it good?" She asked him.

"Hell yeah!"

"I hope you ain't through," she asked caressing his dick trying to get it back hard.

"Naw, I damn sure ain't through," Smurf said before positioning himself between her legs. He entered her slow feeling how warm, wet and tight her pussy was. It felt like her pussy was made especially for his dick.

"Don't break my heart, Smurf," she whispered so softly he barely heard her.

"I won't, baby," he said before starting to move in and out of her.

After a while, he grabbed her legs and pushed them back to her chest and pounded her pussy out. Trina was so wet. Her pussy was making those squishing sounds that was driving him crazy.

"This dick good?"

"Yeah it's good. Hit it from the back so you can slap my ass."

"Get on your knees, face down, ass up, so I can do my thang."

"Don't pull it out when you get ready to nut. Come inside me."

"I planned on doing that anyway," he said, sliding back in her tight pussy."

He started dicking her down like a champ.

Trina, not being fucked in so long, was throwing the pussy right back at him. She was trying to get as many nuts as she could to catch up on all the dick she had missed being single.

When he finally nutted, he felt like he shot a gallon of cum in her pussy. He immediately fell back on the couch exhausted.

"Damn boy, yo' dick game crazy."

"You got some good ass pussy too. I think I'm in love," he mumbled before falling to sleep.

She curled up next to him, sleepy and satisfied and dozed off.

Chapter 16

At the same time Smurf was fucking the shit out of Trina, Robert was in the room next door with Lisa folded up like a pretzel giving her some hard dick.

Sweat was flying off both their bodies and they were both making animal noises as they both tried to fuck the other one to death. Lisa was rotating her hips as Robert pulled all the way out until only the head was still inside her. Then, he slammed his dick inside her so hard the headboard almost broke.

"Gimme that dick nigga. Oh shit, fuck this pussy like you trying to put yo' name on it."

"I'm finna cum in this pussy, Lisa. Throw that shit back, I'm finna nut!"

"Bust that shit daddy. I'm finna cum too. Ohhhhhh, I'm nutting all on that dick. Don't stop, hit it harder. I'm cummingggggggg!"

Robert collapsed on top of her. He was spent. They just laid there breathing hard, trying to regain enough strength to move. Lisa's good ass pussy was too much for Robert. He fell in a dreamless sleep and didn't wake up until four hours later.

By the time he woke up, Lisa had already cooked up three of the bricks out of the ten that Omar gave to Robert. Out of each brick, she put her whip game down and brought back fifty ounces. Omar also gave them fifty thousand X-pills and twenty five pounds of weed so he could get on his feet.

"Damn baby, you been on yo' shit," he said coming out of the bathroom seeing her working.

"After I put this good ass pussy on you and put you to sleep, I decided to come on in here and get this shit done while you was out," she said, teasing him.

"So you got jokes, huh?" He said smiling.

"Naw baby, I ain't got no jokes. I'm just saying the pussy put you to bed."

They both burst out laughing.

"I gotta give you that, you got a bad muthafucka 'tween yo' legs. So, what's the play with this work? How we gon' get it off?"

"We gon' flood my kinfolk nem' out in South Dallas and I'ma take some to my people in Oak Cliff. We can get another spot in the South if you want to or we can help my lil' kinfolk nem' get this shit off. With us helping, we can run the spot twenty four seven."

"That sound like a plan."

While Lisa was in the kitchen whipping the work, Robert was in the living room sacking up twenty dollar bags of weed. He sacked up ten pounds of the weed. After Lisa was through, they cleaned the room and drove to Oak Cliff.

They made it to the Saint James Apartments on Kiest and Easter and went to her uncle's door.

"What's up, Unk?" Lisa said when a tall light skinned man opened the door.

"What's up, Niecy? It's been a long ass time since you been over this way. What you up to?" He asked letting them in.

Robert stepped in the door and saw a lady holding a pistol grip shotgun and a Doberman Pinscher staring at him. Robert stopped behind Lisa and said, "Hey, that dog don't bite, do he?"

"Yeah, she bites if I tell her to or you get rowdy in here. Otherwise, she's an angel."

"Unk, this is my boyfriend Robert. Robert, this is my Uncle Jay but everybody call him Skool."

Robert nodded his head at Skool but he was too busy watching the dog to do a whole lot of talking.

"Hey, Aunt Gail. I didn't even see you sitting over there. That's my Aunt Gail, Aunt Gail this is Robert."

"How you doing?" She asked Robert

"I'm good."

"What brings you to see your Unk?" Skool asked Lisa

"Well Unk, I got some work I'm trying to get off of and I got a connect that prices might be cheaper than what you already paying. I'm trying to front you two bricks already cooked up. You keep forty percent of the profit and give us sixty. Plus, I got a plug on the X-pills and the green for the low-low."

"I need ten pounds and ten thousand pills right now. How much can you get that for?"

"I can get you the pills for two dollars and fifty cent a pill and the Kush gone run you twenty five hundred a pound."

"That's a bet. When can you get it to me?"

"I'll have it in the morning. So have that bread ready and I'll be back early in the morning. I gotta go hit my plug up and get the shit so I'll fuck with you in the morning."

"I'ma give you the bread right now, just have my shit for me in the morning."

"Bet that."

"Baby, go get me fifty thousand outta the safe," Skool told his wife, Gail.

She got up and went to the back room and came back a few minutes later with a bundle of cash.

"That's fifty stacks right there," she said handing the money to him and he handed it to Lisa. She counted it right there in front of them.

"You ain't gotta count my shit, neicy."

"Business is business. I know your money good. That's why I'm over here fucking with you. But, you know how it is when you conducting business. No disrespect Unk.

"Just have my shit over here in the morning and what's up with your mama? She ain't answering the phone."

"Oh, she got her a new boyfriend that she been spending all her time with. She ain't answering my calls either."

"Yeah, well when you talk to her, tell her to call me."

"Alright, I will. I'm 'bout to go to the South and get at your nephews. I'll see you in the morning."

"Alright."

When they got in the car Robert told her, "That was a nice sting you just made."

"I know. Now I need you to call Omar and see how many pounds he'll sell us for that fifty stacks."

"I'll call him as soon as we get back to the room and we need to start looking for a house or something. I'm tired of that room. I want my own shit with a backyard."

"I'll get on it baby."

They made it to the South and found T-Ray, Ant, and Nick sitting on the porch as usual. In the time it took them to park and get out of the car, five customers walked up and got served.

"What up kinfolk and Rob," T-Ray said as they walked up on the porch.

"I see this bitch jumping as usual," Lisa said.

"This bitch will roll twenty four seven, seven days a week if we keep the bitch open. This a million dollar spot. We just can't keep enough work."

"What y'all need?"

"We finna need some more of that Gorilla Piss in an hour or two cause that shit finna be gone and we ran outta X-pills last night. I can't find none nowhere. My connect ain't got none and these other niggas wanna charge too much."

"I got some pills in the car, some Piss and some Kush."

"We need all that. I got that bread ready for y'all too."

"I came over here to holla at you about a business deal if you interested."

"What kind of deal?"

"Like you said you got a million dollar spot but you keep running outta work and missing money. We got the work but no spot to sell it at. We trying to come in with y'all. We go half on everything and split fifty fifty. With us on the team, we can keep this bitch open twenty four seven. Also, with us here every day, y'all niggas can get in the studio with Rob and make some hits."

"Hell yeah," Ant said.

"So we gon' go half on all the work and split everything," T-Ray asked.

"Yeah, we split everything. Plus, we gon' get the cheapest prices in the city on everything," Lisa told him.

"Ant, Nick, what y'all think about that?" T-Ray asked his brothers.

"I'm with that shit. That way we can make some music with Robert. I ain't tryna sell dope all my life. I wanna make a hit and get some industry money," Ant said.

"Me too." Nick added.

"Let's do this shit then."

Lisa went to the car and got three of the bricks she cooked up, the ten pounds that Robert had sacked up and the X-pills. They went in the house and she separated the ten thousand pills she owed Skool and then they started cutting the work up and making powder packs.

Once they got everything situated at the spot, Robert and Lisa drove back to the room to get the rest of the drugs they had stashed in the room.

When they walked in their room, the first thing they heard was beating on the wall coming from Smurf's room.

"What the hell that lil' nigga over there doing?"

"They fucking. That's the headboard banging against the wall. Sounds like he trying to knock the lining outta her little pussy."

Robert walked over to the wall and put his ear against it and listened for a minute. "Yeah, they fucking. You can hear them over there moaning and shit. That little nigga hurting that pussy."

When Robert turned around, Lisa was standing behind him naked.

"You need to be hurting this pussy," she said firing up a Newport dipped in that Gorilla Piss.

Chapter 17

Omar and Junior was in the office at the club counting money and going over the books. They were in the process of opening three more sports bars, but Omar wanted to do something big for the city at the club.

"Junior, we need to do something big to make these niggas know this the spot to be at on the weekends."

"What you wanna do?"

"Shit, I don't know. You part owner and the manager, you ain't got no ideas? Let's do a twerking contest for ten thousand or something."

"Naw, too many people have done that and plus our club is too classy for a twerk contest. How about a player's ball. Christmas is coming up and we can do it on Christmas eve or Christmas night. All the pimps, players, and hustlers in the state of Texas. With good advertisement we can fill this bitch up with the biggest party of the year and have niggas talking about for a whole year," Junior said, getting excited.

"That sounds like a good idea. Let's put it together and see what the budget will be. We got about a month to get everything together, so let's get on it."

"I'm on it. I'ma shut the city down with this party. Watch me work, big bro."

Omar left the club and went to his house where he picked up Em and Kelly and they drove to his mom's old house to meet George McGuire.

He went to the basement and opened the safe and got out several bags stuffed with money and carried them back upstairs. They didn't have to wait long before he pulled up in a van.

Omar carried the bags out to the van and told him, "That's two hundred million. A hundred goes to my account minus your three million and a hundred goes to the old man."

"Check your account in seven days, it should be there."

"Alright, be safe," Omar told him and he drove off.

Omar thought that man gotta be crazy driving around with two hundred million and no bodyguards or security. But Omar didn't know that it was three cars with two highly trained killers in each car that followed Mr. McGuire everywhere he went.

On his way back in the house, his phone started ringing. He looked at the caller ID and saw that it was Robert.

"What's up?" Omar answered.

"Ain't shit, trying to see if I can fuck with you on this fifty stacks."

"What you need."

"That Rick James."

"You say you got fifty?"

"Yeah."

"I can give you twenty five for that."

"Bet."

"When you need them?"

"As soon as you can get them to me."

"I'll slide through in a few hours. I'll call you when I'm on the way. You at the room?"

"Yeah."

"Alright, I'll holla at you in a few."

"One."

When he hung up from Robert, he called Glenn to see what he was up to.

"What up?"

"Just got up. Finna make a few moves to check on a couple of dollars. What you got going on?"

"At the spot. I just gave that bread to the ole boy and I'm finna fuck with Robert on twenty five of them Rick James for fifty stacks."

"You got it or you wanna let me handle it."

"I got it since I'm already over here. But, I'll give him your number and tell him to start fucking with you from now on."

"Yeah, that's cool."

"Me and Junior putting together a players ball on Christmas night at the club so don't make no plans for Christmas. This gon' be the biggest party of the year nigga and you gotta be in the house. If you talk to Jay and Dell before I do, let them niggas know too."

"I got you baby bro. Let me get off this phone and go handle this business."

"Alright, I'll fuck with you later."

Omar hung up the phone and called Big Dre.

"What's up with it?" Dre said, answering the phone.

"What you doing?"

"I'm in Nebraska fucking with my white boys and networking."

"I was just checking on you. I hadn't heard from you in a few days. Oh yeah, don't make no plans for Christmas night. We got some shit in the making. I'll hip you to it when you get back in town."

"Alright, I'll get at you when I get back."

"Alright."

Not long after he hung up, Enrique called.

"What's up ole man?"

"Hey son, you doing okay?"

"I'm good. Everything is okay in the city, business is good and I'm looking for some new spots to open a few more sports bars."

"I got a woman that may be able to help you find the right locations to make a lot of business. I'll tell her to give you a call, okay?"

"Yeah, tell her to give me a call."

"I will. Listen, I just got some disturbing news. I hear your friend Dre is in Nebraska."

"Yeah, I just got off the phone with him. How you know he's in Nebraska?"

"Son, I know almost everything that goes on with the people that's part of my family. Call him immediately and tell him to get out of Nebraska and do not conduct any business with a white guy that goes by the name of John Amos. He's a federal agent."

"You sure Dre is fucking with him?"

"He hasn't did any business with him yet. But, this guy Amos has infiltrated the circle of one of his regular people up there."

"I'm on it."

"Tell him to let his friend Brad know that the guy Amos is a federal agent and needs to be eliminated."

"I'm about to call him right now. I'll hit you back later when I get back home."

"Okay son. Tell Dre his people is safe. I took care of the investigation. But they need to handle that situation as soon as possible."

"I got you."

He hung up and called Big Dre. "Blood, you need to get the fuck outta Nebraska immediately."

"What's going on?"

"Enrique just called and told me that your friend, Brad's circle has been infiltrated by the Feds. Don't do no business with John Amos, he's a federal agent.

"I'm supposed to meet him in a couple of hours."

"Don't meet him. Tell Brad he needs to get rid of that problem. The Fed investigation is dead. But they need to clear those loose ends up."

"I'm on it. I'll hit you when I get back. Tell the ole man I said thanks."

"I got you, get outta there and come home before they do anything."

"I'll be gone within the hour."

"Alright, one."

Omar got off the phone and went back upstairs where Em and Kelly was smoking a blunt.

"What's up? Y'all ready to get outta here?"

"We need to talk to you about something before we go," Em told him with a serious look on her face.

"What's up? Everything good with y'all?"

"Yeah, but, we have a problem."

"Let me know what's up," he said sitting down on the couch.

"We love working for you and you take good care of us and we have all decided that we wanna work with you and your family forever. We know it's certain things we can't do like bringing men into our circle cause of the line of business we are in. but Omar, we need some dick."

"Damn, that's my fault for not thinking about y'all needs. Take a couple of weeks' vacation, pick anywhere y'all wanna go and it's on me."

"We ain't talking about no shit like that. We want some dick from you. All three of us. We know you love Shalika and Zell but you gotta think about us too. We not gonna start catching feelings or any of that, but we all need to be fucked down at least once a week."

Omar was shocked. He had no idea that Em or K-Rock liked dick. He knew all three of them were lesbians and they fucked around with each other. But, they had never gave him any idea they liked men. He would have been fucked the shit outta Em, with her fine ass.

What they didn't know was that Omar had already fucked J-Low in the middle of the Atlantic Ocean. He thought back to the night it all happened.

Zell, Shalika, and J-Low were in the room on the ship playing a game called, Never Have I Ever. Each one of them got a chance to tell something they did that was wild and crazy. If the other two had never did it, then they had to take a shot of Tequila.

It started out simple with J-Low telling she saw a lion in the desert while in the military, in Saudi Arabia. Never had Zell or Shalika ever saw a lion outside of a zoo. They had to take a shot.

J-Low got to go first again. She told them about making bombs while in the military. They had never done that either. They took another shot.

Shalika was feeling the alcohol after several shots and upped the ante. Instead of just a shot, you had to take a clothing item off if you had never ever.

Omar was outside the room at the bar when the game started. By the time he made it back to the room, all three of them were down to their thongs or panties.

"Hey baby, you wanna play?" Zell asked, already tipsy.

"What y'all playing?"

"Never Have I Ever. Each one of us gets to tell something wild we did and if you have never did it, you gotta take a shot and take something off."

Being that they were all women, they decided to team up on Omar and in no time at all had him down to his boxers with questions like sitting down to pee, showing their breasts at Mardi Gras, wearing a thong and other female things they knew he'd never did.

"Y'all cheating, you know I ain't never did no shit like that," Omar said.

"We didn't set no rules on the questions or what we did. If you have never ever, then take those pants off and take this shot," Zell said.

Omar found his self naked not long after. He tried concentrating on the game but couldn't help staring at their breasts and pussy prints. He started to get an erection.

When J-Low looked over and saw his hard dick she said, "Oh my God, look at his dick."

They all bust out laughing and pointing, drunk as hell. A few minutes later, they had a train going. Shalika was eating out Zell, J-Low was eating Shalika out and he was deep in J-Low pussy doggy style.

J-Low pussy was so tight, wet and warm. He almost nutted as soon as he entered her. But, he fought it off and started fucking the shit outta her. Her pussy was so wet, creamy, white cum was dripping off his dick.

Before the night was over, he had fucked and sucked every pussy in the room. He even fucked J-Low up in the ass while Zell and Shalika were passed out sleep.

At the same time Omar was having his thoughts, Kelly was doing the same thing. She was thinking about the night she spent in the room with Faye and Pops, his mom and dad, on that same ship.

"Is J-Low in on this little ploy?" Omar asked.

"Yeah, we talked to her and she agrees with us."

"So how y'all think we should do this?"

"We can start with you fucking us today and then once a week you can take us one a day. Take Kelly to the back and fuck her then I'm next."

Omar took Kelly to the back bedroom and knocked the lining outta her tight pussy. Kelly was a screamer and a runner. He had to pin her down against the headboard to put the pound game down.

In twenty minutes, Kelly had already had five orgasms and tapped out. She grabbed her clothes and ran out the room to go shower. He told her to send Em in.

Em came in the door getting out of her clothes. He knew Em was their leader so he knew he had to put it down on her. When she was naked, he pushed her to her knees and grabbed the back of her head and guided it to his dick. He fucked her mouth for a good fifteen minutes. Em had that good sloppy head.

He finally climbed between her legs and put the head in her. For a good two or three minutes, he fucked her by just putting the head in and out of her pussy.

"Shit, that feels good," Em moaned.

He started slow fucking her with long hard strokes. Her pussy was making those wet sounds every time he went all the way in. He got on his knees and pushed her legs all the way back and really started giving her the dick. Fast, slow, pound game, slow, long stroke, pound game.

"You fucking the shit outta this pussy. I knew you was gone have some good dick. I'm finna nut again, Oh shit, I'm cumming."

He flipped her over and started fucking her from the back. Her pussy was leaking like a faucet. He stuck his hand under her pussy and came away with his hand soaked in pussy juice. He rubbed the pussy juice on her asshole and pushed his middle finger inside.

Instantly, a warm wetness shot outta her pussy and continued squirting outta her for the next ten seconds.

"Oh shit, I can't stop cumming."

She fell face first on the bed as soon as she stopped cumming, Omar dick slid out of her still hard as a rock.

"Sit down right here. I'ma suck that dick."

She sucked his dick until he came down her throat and they got cleaned up and went back home.

Omar played with Omari, Shayla, King and Queen for a while before he went into the bedroom and laid down to take a nap. Not long after he closed his eyes, Zell was waking him up.

"Omar, you need to come down stairs, there's a little boy down there that looks just like you and he says you are his father."

"A what?"

"Come on," she said, pulling him outta the room.

They made it down stairs and just like Zell said there was a little boy, six or seven years old, that looked just like him.

Omar knew immediately who the little boy's mother was. He could see her features in his face as well as his own.

The boy was light complected, with the same eyes, nose and lips as Omar. He even had the same dimple Omar had on his left cheek.

Tari Johnson, Ms. Johnson or J, from the prison. The guard he was fucking. He could hear her voice as if it was yesterday.

"Ohhhhhhhhh Omar, I'ma miss this good ass dick. Take that condom off and fill this pussy with sweet nut." She reached down and snatched the condom off and put his dick right back inside of her. "Now beat this pussy up like you promised."

He looked at the boy and the boy was looking at him with the same intensity.

"Yo mama name is Tari?"

The boy nodded his head. Omar smiled and the little boy blushed.

"How old are you?"

"Six."

He asked that so Zell could hear the age of the boy and know that this happened before he met her.

"What's your name?"

"Omar Wilson Junior. But everybody calls me Junior. Are you my daddy?"

"Yeah, I think so? Where yo mama at?"

"She gave me a letter to give to you. It's in my suitcase, I'll go get it," he said running in the other room. He came back with a sealed envelope a few minutes later.

Omar opened the envelope and found the boy's social security card, birth certificate and a book with the records of his immunization shots. A handwritten letter was the last thing in the envelope.

He opened the letter and read.

'Omar, I'm sorry that you had to find out about our son like this. I never intended to tell you, but shit happens. I have terminal cancer that has spread to my liver and kidneys. Doctors are giving me a very short time to live. I have sent Junior to you so that he can be with his father. I am putting my parents' contact info and I have given my mom your contact info. Take care of Junior, he loves you. I have always talked to him about you. I will see you and him on the other side.'

With love,

J

Omar passed the letter to Zell and Shalika so they could read it.

"Well, I guess we better find you a room," Omar said.

"I'ma stay here in this house, with you? I wanna stay here. But I didn't know if you wanted me cause you my daddy but you never came around."

"Son, I never knew you was alive until today. You mom never told me I had a son."

"My mama never told you about me?"

"Nope. But now that I know you are my son, we gonna have lots of fun together. These are my wife's Zell and Shalika. These your sisters Omari, Shayla and that's your big sister, Danielle. Y'all, this is little Omar. We gonna call you little Omar alright, lil' man?"

"Yeah, that's alright daddy. Can me and Shayla go play the video game now?"

"Yeah, go ahead."

"His mother was a prison guard that I was messing with while I was locked up. I didn't even know she was pregnant."

"He's part of our family now. Let's go find him a room. What about the room across the hall from Shayla?" Zell said.

They grabbed his suitcase and took it down the hallway across from Shayla.

Chapter 18

Yogi was fucked up. He couldn't sleep. He was nervous as fuck and paranoid. Pam tried consoling him but nothing seemed to work except alcohol and weed.

The night he shot up Dee-Man's mama house, one of the bullets struck Dee-Man's sister's little girl in the head, killing her in her sleep. The little girl was only three years old.

Yogi felt sick to his stomach. He couldn't get the picture out of his head of a beautiful, smiling little girl, they'd shown on the news. He knew without a doubt that one of the bullets he fired took her life and he was heartbroken. He never wanted to see another gun, much less shoot one.

"I gotta get outta this city, Pam. I can't stay here no more. It's too many fucked up memories, too much violence. I just wanna live a quiet life with you and watch our children grow up."

"I'm with you baby no matter what you wanna do," Pam assured him.

"I own a small little ranch in Colorado. That's where I'm going, to Colorado where I ain't gotta worry about nothing but my family and the animals on the ranch. Will you come with me baby?"

"I already told you I would. When are we leaving?"

"We can leave tonight. Let me make a few calls and I'll be ready to leave."

"I need to call a few people too," she said going to the bedroom to get her phone so she could call Trina.

"What's up girl?" Trina answered.

"We about to get outta Texas. Yogi don't wanna be down here no more. He been stressing ever since Dee-Man sister Sarah, baby was killed. He said he tired of all this killing and violence. He just wanna be somewhere safe so we can raise our kids."

"You pregnant?"

"Naw, not yet. But we been working on it."

"Well, I'm happy for you. Stay in touch and we'll come visit."

"You know I am. I'm so glad we both found some good men and some happiness. We deserve to be happy."

"I know girl. Be careful and call me when you get where you are going."

"We are going to Colorado. Yogi owns a small ranch up there so we gon' go live on his ranch. I'll call you when we get there," she said, hanging up.

Yogi had twelve rent houses that he rented out to people on Section 8. He told them his new address and did a few other odds and ends before he went to the bedroom and emptied out his safe.

He had eight hundred thousand in cash in the safe. He packed it in one of his bags and the two matching nine millimeter pistols with four extra clips.

He took the bags to the garage and loaded their stuff in his truck. He went back through the house turning off lights and locking windows and doors. They got in the truck and drove off, headed straight for the interstate to Colorado.

Chapter 19

Smurf was chilling in the room smoking a blunt watching ESPN. He had just finished fucking the shit outta Trina. She was in the bedroom sleeping. He heard someone knocking on the door. He looked through the peephole and saw that it was Robert and Lisa. He opened the door.

"What y'all up to?" He asked letting them in the room.

"Ain't shit, just stop by to check on y'all."

"Where Trina at?" Lisa asked.

"She taking a nap."

"We heard y'all trying to knock a hole in the wall. The way that headboard was banging against the wall. Y'all was doing some serious fucking," Lisa said laughing.

"Naw, we was cleaning the room up." Smurf tried to lie.

"Yeah right," They both said.

"We finna head to the south. We found a little spot with Lisa kinfolks that we can hustle out of. I was trying to see if y'all wanna ride with us."

"Let me go wake Trina up and see if she wanna ride. I'm tired of sitting in this room."

He went to the bedroom. Trina was laying across the bed in only her panties half covered by the sheets. He slapped her on the ass.

"Ouch, stop Smurf."

"Get up and let's take a ride with Lisa and Robert to the south."

"I gotta take a shower real fast."

"You want me to get in with you?"

"You know if you get in the shower with me what's going to happen."

"Ain't nothing gonna happen."

"You gon' be tryna get some and we gon' end up back in the bed."

"Naw, I'ma control myself. Go turn the water on. I'm on my way."

He went back in the front room and told them, "We gotta hit the shower, give us about fifteen or twenty minutes."

"Come to the room when y'all get ready," Robert said before they left and went back to their room.

Smurf went back in the bathroom where Trina was already in the shower. He got undressed and got in the shower with her.

"I thought you was gon' wait on me?"

"I knew you were coming right back. Look at you, already getting hard. I knew this wasn't a good idea."

"Just a little quickie."

"That's what yo' lips say," she said bending over giving him access to her goodies.

Twenty minutes later, they were dressed and knocking on Lisa and Robert's door.

"Y'all ready." Smurf asked as Lisa opened the door and let them in.

"We waiting on y'all."

They went outside and got in Robert's car and drove to Oak Cliff. Lisa got out the car and ran in to go drop the rest of the work off they owed Skool and then they drove to South Dallas.

They spot was jumping as usual when they pulled up. Just before they got out, a dark blue Benz pulled into the driveway three houses down.

"Baby, that looks like Dee-Man car," Trina said, grabbing his arm to stop him from getting out the car.

He looked at the car and said, "That is that nigga car. I wonder what the fuck he doing over here."

"Who is Dee-Man?" Robert asked.

"That's the nigga who killed my mama and my brother," Smurf said watching Dee-Man, Blue Nose and Mookie get out the car and go in the house.

"This nigga been hiding over here the whole time," Smurf said.

"What's up with this nigga? You tryna get at him or what because we can handle that right now," Robert said.

"Naw, it's broad daylight. I know where the nigga at now. He good as dead."

They got out the car and hurried inside so that if they were looking out the window they wouldn't see Smurf or Trina. When they got inside, Lisa introduced them to Ant, T-Ray, and Nick. then, Robert asked, "Who them niggas is that stay three houses down that drive that blue Benz?"

"Them niggas just moved in about a month ago. It was an old lady who lived there but she died. Them niggas see us every day and ain't never spoke to us. You know them niggas."

"Yeah, them niggas killed my nigga brother and his mama."

"Shit, let's air them niggas out," Nick said.

"Them niggas good as got," Smurf said, still looking out the window.

He pulled out his phone and hit Yaki up.

"What the haps?" Yaki answered.

"I just found this nigga Dee-Man and he got them niggas Blue Nose and Mookie with him."

"I'm on my way. Where you at?"

"Chill nigga. It's daylight. I'll call you tonight so be ready."

"I'm always ready to murk something."

"I'ma hit you later on."

"Alright, one."

"One."

A few hours later, Smurf saw Jo-Jo pull up in a black Malibu, get out and go in.

"Jo-Jo just went over there too," Smurf told Trina.

"Who is Jo-Jo?" Robert asked.

"That's my brother old girl. She fucking with the opps now."

"Fuck that hoe. She gon' get it too," Lisa said.

"That goes without saying," Smurf answered.

When it got dark, Smurf called Yaki and told him where he was at. Thirty minutes later, Yaki pulled up dressed in all black in a stolen truck. They sat in the front room watching the house trying to come up with a plan.

"Let's just go over there and light the whole house up," Yaki said.

"Naw, we gonna end this shit tonight. We gon' do this shit smart. We ain't gon' run up on no wild, wild west shit. My nigga nem got this spot and we ain't gon' bring no heat on them. Let's just keep watching and catch them niggas slippin'," Smurf said.

A few minutes later, they watched as Mookie and Blue Nose came out and got in the Benz and drove off.

"Let's follow them niggas," Smurf said running out the door with Robert and Yaki right behind him. They jumped in the stolen truck and followed them to the Williams Chicken on MLK.

Mookie got out and went inside while Blue Nose stayed in the driver's seat.

"I can walk right up on the car and blast that nigga Blue Nose right now," Yaki said.

"Naw, this parking lot lit up and I bet they got some cameras around this bitch somewhere," Robert said.

"Let's wait and see if we get a better shot," Smurf said.

Mookie came back out with several bags and they drove off. Right before he turned on the street that would have took them back to the house, he turned in the parking lot of the corner of Malcolm X and Linway. The parking lot was dark and the nearest street light was almost a half a block away.

"We got these niggas," Yaki said parking on Linway.

"Robert, you get in the driver's seat so you can pull off when we get back to the truck," Smurf said.

"I'm on it, go handle that business."

Smurf and Yaki ran back up to the store and stood in the shadows until they saw Mookie coming back out the store. Smurf ran up on him and let off four shots in his face.

Boom, boom, boom, boom!

Just as Yaki sprayed the driver's side window of the car with that Drako. Smurf ran up on Mookie and let off three more shots in his chest, while Yaki ran up and continued firing shots into the car.

"Let's go!" Smurf said and they ran around the corner and jumped in the truck. Robert pulled off with the headlights off until they got a few blocks away. Then, he hit the headlights and drove a couple of blocks to see if anyone was following them. When he saw the coast was clear, he headed to the spot. He parked the truck on the next block over and they ran through a backyard, hopped a fence and walked down the alley until they came to the backyard of the spot. They went through the gate and went around to the front and went inside the house.

"I'm 'bout to go over here and finish this shit tonight," Smurf said.

"Let's go handle this shit," Robert added.

"I'm down for whatever."

"We really need some heat with silencers on them," Smurf said.

"This the South. Ain't nobody gon' call the laws about hearing gunshots. We hear gunshots every night."

"Let's do this shit then," Smurf said heading to the door.

They went out the house to the backyard and down the alley until they came to the house. They went through the backyard and started looking through the windows.

They looked in one of the windows on the side of the house and saw Dee-Man and Jo-Jo fucking like two rabbits. Jo-Jo had her legs on Dee-Man's shoulders. He was pounding away in her pussy, and she was throwing it back every stroke.

"Look at that fine ass bitch throwing that pussy back," Yaki whispered.

"Let's go to the other side of the house and see if a window is unlocked. They ain't gon' hear shit with all that fucking they doing," Robert said.

They went to the other side of the house and checked the windows. Every window they checked was locked. But, Smurf started removing the putty from one of the windows and in no time had removed the whole window pane. He reached in and unlocked the window.

They listened for a minute before they all climbed in. They were in a small bedroom with the door closed. Robert went to the door and cracked it open and peeped into the hallway. They could hear Jo-Jo moaning and telling Dee-Man to fuck her harder.

"Let's go. They still fucking," Robert said.

They went down the hallway, following the sounds of fucking until they came to the room where the sounds were coming from.

Robert turned the doorknob and pushed the door open. Dee-Man was still pounding Jo-Jo back out. Jo-Jo had her eyes open and was watching them as they came in the room. She smiled and winked at them as they came in the room.

"You got company," she said, pushing Dee-Man off of her.

He looked and saw the three intruders and said, "Oh shit." He dived for the nightstand where his gun was laying but Robert hit him with several haymakers while Yaki grabbed the gun. Jo-Jo just laid there with her legs open and pussy juice glistening off her thighs and pussy.

"Big Tiger told me to tell you, loyalty over everything," Jo-Jo said to Smurf.

Smurf stood there letting the message register in his mind for a few seconds before he finally said, "Get dressed Jo-Jo and get out of here."

Jo-Jo jumped off the bed, found her clothes, and started getting dressed.

"You got some good dick, Dee-Man. Sorry you ain't gon' be able to use it no more," she said laughing as she walked out the room.

"Get something to tie this nigga up with," Robert said, still holding Dee-Man down.

Smurf grabbed the sheet off the bed and tied his feet, then they tied his hands behind his back.

"Take his punk ass to the bathtub," Smurf said.

"You might as well kill me. I ain't gon' do no begging or apologizing. It is what it is. Where my lil' niggas at?"

"They at the same place you finna be. DEAD!" Smurf told him.

They carried him into the bathroom and dumped him in the tub. Smurf grabbed a pillow off the bed and followed them.

"This for my mama and my brother, bitch ass nigga," Smurf said, wrapping the pillow around the pistol to somewhat muffle the sound and firing eight shots into Dee-Mans head and back.

"We gon' wrap him up, put him in that truck and dump the truck."

It's a Minyard's right up the street. I'll park that bitch in the parking lot," Yaki said.

"Alright, go get the truck," Smurf told him.

On his way to the front door, he saw a duffle bag on the couch. He looked inside and saw it was filled with money. He picked it up and went back in the bathroom and dropped it at Smurf's feet.

"Look at all this money." He left to go get the truck.

"Let's find something to wrap him up in," Robert said.

They found some sheets and blankets in one of the rooms and wrapped the body up in them. When Yaki came back, they carried him out to the truck. Yaki got in and drove off.

Smurf and Robert went back in the house to clean up. They ran water and bleach down the drain in the tub and wipe the walls down with bleach soaked towels. Yaki came back just as they were finishing. "I parked the truck at Minyard's."

"Let's get the fuck outta here. Don't forget that money," Robert said and they left.

Smurf sat out on the porch smoking a blunt when they got back to the spot. Trina came out and sat with him and asked," Is it over?"

"Yeah, it's over."

"Good."

Later, when Robert, Nick and Ant went to the homemade studio, Smurf went with them. They started kicking around freestyles over a beat and Smurf grabbed the mic. That was the night they found out he could rap and added him to the group.

Chapter 20

It was Christmas night and Omar had his whole family and crew at the club he owned with his little brother Junior. Shalika was weeks away from having their baby. But she couldn't miss the Christmas party. Her and Zell had on matching Ralph Lauren hip hugging dresses. Zell's was black and Shalika's was white.

J-Low, K-Rock and Em all had on dresses or miniskirts that showed off their figures. The way J-Lows ass was shaking in her mini shirt, he could tell she didn't have on any panties. 'Damn, that girl fine,' he thought. 'Look at them big ass, pretty, brown titties bout to bust out the top of her dress.'

He had to admit that Zell was the sexiest outta all the women that was with him. The way her dress was hugging her ass and the top of the dress barely held her titties in. She had been hitting the home gym every morning since she'd had Omari and it paid off.

Faye and Pops came in and Omar had to turn his head from staring at his mom. She had on a long red dress that showed off every curve of her ass and she had a bunch of ass. Connie came in wearing a low cut jeans outfit with the top part of her thong showing. Her ass was so fat it looked like she had something on her back.

They were in the private VIP room where they could look out over the club and dance floor. Omar had on a brown Gucci fit with his chains on. His neck looked like a rainbow. He had on his MOB chain with red diamonds, a chain with a seven pendant flooded in yellow and white diamonds and a chain with a 22 on it in black diamonds.

As they sat around talking, Junior came in the room leading Sharhonda and her sister Yolonda, Omar's old girlfriend.

"Look who I ran into," Junior said.

"Yolonda."

"Shalika."

They jumped up and ran into each other's arms. "Girl, I haven't seen you in a long time. I see you on TV all the time. You back home to stay?"

"Naw, we just back for the holidays," she said, staring at Omar.

"Let me introduce you, this is Zell, my wife in law. These are our friends J-Low, Em and K-Rock and this is our husband, Omar."

"Hi, how are y'all. I'm Yolonda and this is my sister Sharhonda."

"Hey Omar," Sharhonda said.

"Y'all already know Omar?" Shalika asked.

"Yeah, him and Sharhonda's old boyfriend was cool," Yolonda answered.

Omar was looking at Yolonda and thinking to his self, 'It look like that ass done got fatter. She still looking good too.'

Shalika, Yolonda, and Sharhonda had moved to a table and was talking about old times. Glenn, Dell, and Jay walked in.

"What up, fam?" Glenn said. He was with his girlfriend Carmen. Carmen was a Spanish girl that Glenn had been messing with for years.

Dell and Jay always came alone. They both thought they were players and vowed to be single forever.

"What up lil' bro?" Jay asked, hugging him.

"Same ole, same ole."

After they spoke to everyone, Dell asked, "Ain't that Yolonda over there with Shalika?"

"Yeah, that's her."

"She still looking good. How you pull that off? You still been fucking with her?"

"Bro, I haven't seen or talked to her but once or twice since she left. Her and Sharhonda just showed up. Junior brought them up here."

Faye walked up as they were talking.

"Hey mama," Jay and Dell said, giving her a hug.

"How y'all doing?" She said hugging them while staring at Omar. "Why the hell you got that girl up in here with Shalika and Zell?"

"Mama, Junior brought them up here. I didn't even know she was in Dallas."

"Well, that's your problem. I'm not gon' let you ruin my night."

Robert and Lisa along with Smurf and Tina, Smurf with his fake I.D. came in. As soon as the DJ saw Robert, he threw on his hit, The Lane and the whole club got crunk and started dancing and celebrating.

Omar saw J-Don with four of his girls and went over to speak to him.

"What's up? Merry Christmas, my nigga."

"Merry Christmas to you too. What's been going on?"

"Ain't much," Omar answered.

"I'ma give you a call sometime next week. I need to holla at you on some business."

"Fuck with me, you got the number."

"Alright."

Omar walked around the club seeing old faces and some new ones too. As he got close to the entrance, he saw one of his old friends who had told Enrique about him Rudy Martinez and his best friend and Sharhonda's old boyfriend, Todd. He walked over and shook their hands.

"What up?"

"Trying to enjoy this Christmas night," Rudy answered.

"You at the right spot. You know we gon' do it big tonight. What up Todd? Sharhonda up in VIP with Yolonda and my family. Come on, I'll take y'all up there."

They started walking towards the private VIP room when Rudy said, "I been hearing big thangs coming outta your camp."

"Oh yeah, 'preciate the plug."

"No need to thank me. I know you are about your business."

He dropped them off at the VIP room and headed back out to the club. Not long after, the Fire Marshall came in and shut the party down. He said the club was over packed.

They headed back to Omar's house and continued to celebrate. The whole family followed them to the house. Shalika invited Yolonda and Sharhonda and Omar invited Rudy and Todd to come and party with them. But, both Rudy and Todd had to go see their families. Sharhonda went with Rudy and Todd but, Yolonda decided to come spend time and party with Shalika. They hadn't saw each other in years. By the time Shalika got back from college, Yolonda was already in California.

They got to the house, threw on some Christmas carols, told stories, and enjoyed the holiday.

When Omar was able to get Yolonda alone he whispered, "That's still my pussy."

"When you gon' show me it's still yours?"

"Soon," he said before walking off before Zell or Shalika saw them whispering. He walked off knowing that it was just a matter of time before he got back between her legs.

Chapter 21

Smurf and Trina had bought a four bedroom house with Robert and Lisa. He flooded his whole hood with work and let the homies from his block sell it. His bank was getting right. The new year had come and that was his whole mission for the new year, to get the bag.

He was awake but he was just lying in the bed relaxing next to Trina. He looked at the clock and saw that it was 9:25 am. Trina's warm body was against his. Just when he was about to roll over and slide inside her, his phone started ringing. He reached over on the nightstand got his phone and answered.

"Yeah."

"Bro, these pigs just arrested me for murder."

"Who you kill nigga?"

"My nigga, I ain't killed nobody. They arrested me for Dee-Man murder."

"How the fuck they get you for Dee-Man murder?" Smurf asked, then added. "That dirty bitch Jo-Jo."

"Naw, these phones recorded so be careful. But the surveillance cameras at the Minyard's saw me park the truck that they found his body in. I told them hoes I don't know shit about no body. Some niggas gave me two hundred dollars to park the truck."

"Don't even talk to them hoes no more. I'm finna call Omar and get you a lawyer. They gave you a bond yet?"

"Nigga, I'm at the juvenile detention center. Ain't no bonds in juvenile."

"Bro, let me call Omar and we gon' get right on top of this shit. Don't talk to them hoes no more. Just because you parked the truck don't mean shit. Just chill, I'm finna call Omar. We gon' get you outta that bitch."

"Alright. I'll hit you back later tonight and see what the deal is."

"Alright."

He ended the call and started calling Omar when Trina asked, "What happened?"

"The laws got Yaki for Dee-Man's murder. The cameras got him parking the truck that they found his body in."

"They not gonna come looking for you, are they?"

"Naw, my nigga solid. He ain't gon' tell them hoes shit."

"Yo, Omar, the laws just arrested Yaki for Dee-Man murder. They got him at the juvenile. You know any good lawyers?"

"Somebody talking."

"Naw, the cameras got Yaki parking the truck that they found the body in."

"Let me call my attorney and get him on top of it. I'ma come through and holla at you in a couple of hours."

"Alright."

He hung up the phone and told Trina, "Everything is good they can't prove he killed the nigga because he parked the truck. Omar finna get a lawyer down there. Let me go holla at Robert."

He got up and went down the hall to Robert's door and knocked. "Come on in," Robert answered.

"My nigga, the laws just got Yaki for Dee-Man's murder."

"That punk ass bitch. I knew we shoulda smoked her too," Robert said getting out of bed. "Lisa, get up baby and pack, we finna get the fuck outta Texas."

"Naw my nigga, that bitch ain't said shit. The laws ain't on us."

"Then, how the fuck they got Yaki? Don't nobody else know shit but us four."

"The cameras in the parking lot got Yaki parking the truck."

"Fuck! I shoulda knew them stores got cameras. Especially in the South where the crime rate is so high."

"He told the laws some niggas paid him to park the truck."

"That's good. They can't prove he killed the nigga just because he parked the truck. We gotta get that nigga a lawyer down there and he need to stop talking to them detectives."

"Omar sending a lawyer down there and I told him not to talk to them hoes no more."

"We gon' go visit the lil' nigga later today. Where he at, Lew Sterrett?"

"Naw, the nigga in juvenile. The nigga only sixteen."

"That's better than being in the county jail. We gon' go see the nigga later. Call the juvenile and see when visiting hours."

"I'ma get Trina to do it. I'll let you know," he said heading back to his room.

Trina called and got the visiting hours and a couple of hours later, Omar was knocking on the door.

"What up?" Smurf asked, opening the door.

"The lawyer on it," Omar said, closing the door. "If all Yaki told the laws was that some niggas paid him to park the truck he might be good. The lawyer gon' check and see what all he said. Let's go see the nigga."

They drove to the juvenile center in West Dallas and went in. Twenty minutes later, Yaki walked in the visiting room.

"What up nigga?" Smurf said hugging his homie.

"Ain't shit. These hoes tryna take a nigga off the pavement."

"The lawyer should be down here to see you soon. He already on it," Omar said.

116

"He already called down here and had them call me out and I talked to him on the phone," Yaki told them.

"That's good. He on his shit then," Omar said.

"How much the lawyer charge you? Cause me and Smurf can pay you back," Robert said

"Y'all good, I got it," Omar said.

"Where they arrest you at?" Smurf asked.

"Nigga, I was at my mama house sleep. She came and woke me up and said they had the house surrounded and the whole street blocked off. Then, them dumb ass laws get on a bullhorn and call my whole name out and tell me to come out the house with my hands up. Mama was scared as fuck."

"I'ma put some money on your books so you can get the shit you need," Smurf told him.

"Naw, I'm good. They put the money I had on me on my books. But, go through the hood and get that bread from them niggas at the spot. They should have twenty five stacks and get them niggas some more work over there. I had to flush the shit I had and you already know mama was mad as a muthafucka. She wanted to smoke that."

"I got you and I'ma take mama something over there to hold her over."

"She gon' appreciate that and let her know I'm good. I called her but she be talking to reckless on the phone and you know they listening."

"I got you," Smurf said.

A few minutes later, a detention center officer came in and told them they time was up. They all hugged Yaki and told him to keep his head up and left.

When they got outside, Omar saw that he had several missed calls from Enrique. He called him back.

"What's up, ole man?"

"Hey son, call me from the good phone."

"I'm not at the house right now. But, give me about an hour and I'll call you."

"Okay, I'll be waiting."

Omar dropped Smurf and Robert off and headed straight to the house.

Chapter 22

Omar went in the house and found Marie. "Get the old man on the phone for me."

They went to the basement and Marie made the call and handed him the phone.

"Hey son, how are you?"

"I'm good."

"Okay, I'm at my residence in Florida but I will be returning to Colombia today. There is a lot going on back home. We are at war with some guys that are getting greedy and trying to move into places that don't concern them. I have loaded your storage places up. Things may get crazy for a minute. If by any chance that anything should happen to me, you don't owe anything. Just make sure that my sister and her people are taken care of."

"Your sister? Is she in Texas?"

"Yes, she's in Texas. Matter of fact, she lives with you."

"Marie?"

"Yes, Marie is my baby sister. She is not a legal citizen, but she has been here most of her life. Plus, I have willed my Florida residence to you if anything should happen to me."

"Uh, thanks. The situation over there is serious then?"

"Very serious."

"Well, I promise you that Marie and her family will always have a place with me and they will be very well taken care of. Is there anything that I can do to help?"

"There are billions of dollars being made from the products Colombia produces. The Mexican cartels got involved years ago and made it easier for us to distribute our products. Now, everybody wants a piece of the pie. The cartels are fighting, the Colombians are fighting also. This is the way of life. The wolves prey on the weak, only the strong survive. Remember that son, only the strong survive. Build you an army and keep your soldiers content and happy and they will give their life for you. This, my father taught me when I was a small boy."

"I will take your wisdom and apply it to my everyday life," Omar said.

"I will talk to you later, son. I have a plane to catch."

"Okay old man. Take care and be safe."

"I will, son."

Omar ended the call, called Glenn, and told him everything.

"Check the storage."

"I'm at the storage right now. Bro, this bitch is loaded. This is like twenty times what we normally get. It must be more serious than what he's telling you."

"I don't know. All we can do is just continue to do us and let them work on the other part."

"Yeah, you right."

"I'ma get at you later."

Omar ended the call and went back upstairs. Lil' Omar and Shayla were playing the video game and he went in and played the game with them.

They were laughing and having fun when Shalika and Zell came in with Little Omari.

"I see y'all are having fun," Zell said.

"And they didn't even invite us," Shalika added.

"I already beat both of y'all," Shayla said.

"Who you beat?" Zell asked.

"You and you," Shayla said laughing.

"I don't remember that," Zell said.

"Me either." Shalika added.

"Alright, y'all three against me and Lil' Omar. What you think about that Lil' Omar? Me and you against them, let's kick they butts."

"Yeah ain't gon' beat nobody. It's three of us against two of y'all. We gon' win," Shayla said.

"Okay, since y'all think y'all gon' win, would y'all like to put a friendly little wager on it?" Omar asked.

"Make it light on yourself, tough guy," Zell said

"If we win, y'all take us to lunch anywhere we wanna go and if y'all win we'll take y'all anywhere y'all wanna go."

"That's a bet!" Shalika said.

"Also, if we win—" Zell whispered in his ear.

"That's a bet! That's a bet!"

"We got this. Come on Shayla, let's kick they butts. Girl power!" She yelled, sticking her hand out for some dap.

"Girl power!" Shayla and Zell yelled.

Two hours later, after losing every game, Omar was in the shower getting ready to take the girls out to eat when Zell and Shalika bust in naked.

"On your knees tough guy, time to pay up," Zell said, putting one of her legs on the side of the tub. Shalika did the same thing. When Zell whispered in his ear before they started the game, she bet him some head.

"Come on y'all, right now?"

"Right now, pay up," They both said massaging their clits.

"Y'all dead wrong," he said dropping to his knees.

Chapter 23

Two weeks later, Shalika was in the hospital giving birth to a seven pound baby girl that she named Omahji. Omar was in the delivery room again, a little more prepared for what was to come than he was the first time.

When the doctor put her in his arms, he couldn't do nothing but smile at how pretty she was. She stared at him and he stared at her.

"I'm your father Omahji."

She just stared at him kicking her little legs, crying. He put her on his shoulder and held her until she stopped crying. He handed her over to Shalika.

"She look just like you," she said smiling.

"Naw, she look like you. Thank you baby for giving me another beautiful little girl."

"Thank you too, for giving me a beautiful little girl."

A few days later, Shalika and the baby was at home. They put Omahji in the crib with her sister.

"They look so cute together," Zell said.

"They do, don't they."

"Omari, meet your little sister Omahji," Zell told her.

Omar stood to the side watching his two daughters with Lil' Omar standing on the side of him with Shayla.

"Y'all come meet your little sister," Omar said.

"I wanna hold her." Lil' Omar said.

Shalika picked her up and put her in his arms." You gotta put your hand behind her head. Always make sure you hold her head."

"Let me hold her too," Shayla said.

They sat around playing with the babies until they both fell asleep. Danielle came down to the nursery and played with her sisters for a while too.

Omar looked at his phone and saw that he had a missed call from Big Dre. He called him back.

"What's up?"

"Ain't shit, just wanted to let you know that that little piece of business in Nebraska has been took care of."

"Enough said. How everything else going?"

"As usual. Glenn told me he got something else for me so I'ma get with him later on today and see what's up. What you got going on?"

"Ain't too much, I been chilling and spending time with my babies."

"That's good. Well bro, I'ma catch up with you later on. I need to make a few moves."

"Alright, be careful," Omar said before ending the call and calling Glenn.

"What up lil' bro?" Glenn said, answering the phone.

"Just checking on you."

"I'm good. But, you need to get your boy to come pick up the money and do his thing. It's piling up."

"Damn, I forgot all about that, with Shalika having the baby and everything. I'ma get on top of that right after I get off the phone with you. Every thang else good."

"Smooth as a baby's ass," Glenn said laughing.

"Alright then, I'ma call my boy so he can pick up that bread I'll get back at you later."

"Alright."

Omar called and made arrangements for him to pick up the money. Then, he went to his bedroom to take a nap.

Yaki was in court with his lawyer having a hearing to see if the state had enough evidence to hold him on a murder charge. He was on the stand being questioned by his attorney.

"Can you tell the court exactly what you were doing in the area the night you were asked to park the truck?" His attorney asked.

"I had caught the bus to South Dallas to go to the State Fair. I got off the bus on Malcolm X and started walking towards the fair. I saw two dudes on the corner of Pennsylvania, and they called me over. They asked me if I could drive and I told them yeah. One of them told me that his brother had stolen a truck and he wanted to get it away from there. They told me they would give me two hundred dollars if I drove the truck somewhere and parked it. I needed the money so I could enjoy myself at the fair so I took the money and drove the truck to the Minyard's and parked it."

"What did you do after you got out of the truck?" His attorney asked.

"I went into the Minyard's and bought a cold drink and some cigarettes."

"Have you talked to the guys who paid you to park the truck or saw them since."

"No sir."

"Your Honor, I would like to admit into evidence video footage of my client parking the truck and going into the store and several minutes later coming out and walking in the direction to the Fair Park. Also, Your Honor I would like to bring to the court's attention that it would have been impossible for my client to carry the body of the victim to the truck. Since we know that he wasn't killed in the truck."

The judge sat there looking at the autopsy report and other papers before he asked, "Do the prosecutors have anything to say?"

"Sir," The prosecutor said, addressing Yaki. "Would you recognize the two guys that paid you to park the truck if you saw them again?"

"Probably."

"Would you take a look at some photos to see if you could identify the guys that paid you to park the truck?"

"No sir."

"Can I ask you why not?"

"If the police would have treated me like they would treat someone from North Dallas or the suburbs, I might have. But, my whole family was embarrassed. It was almost twenty officers surrounding my mom's house with guns drawn and automatic weapons on a bullhorn screaming and shouting. My mom and little sister were terrified. I can't see cooperating with a racist system that has no respect for black people."

"No further questions."

"Well," the judge said. "After hearing the evidence I'm going to have to agree with the defense. There just isn't enough evidence to hold Mr. Anderson. I think it would have been impossible for him to kill the victim, then carry him out to the truck and then drive the truck to its final destination.

"Another thing, from the video, after he parks the truck, he got out and went inside the store. He doesn't look paranoid or worried. He looks like a kid who just made two hundred dollars and he's about to enjoy his night at the fair park.

"Your Honor, he's not being cooperative. He knows more than he's telling us," the prosecutor said.

"So you want me to hold him in jail until he decides to tell you what you want to hear?" The judge stared at the prosecutor waiting on him to respond. "The charges are dropped and the defendant is free to go," the judge said and walked off the bench and out the courtroom.

An hour later, Yaki walked out the juvenile and into Omar's truck where Smurf, Robert, and Omar were waiting.

"Let's get the fuck away from here," he said getting in the truck and closing the door.

***

A week later, Omar was at the spot loading bags of money into George McGuire's van. When he got through loading the money, Mr. McGuire told him, "Check your account in a few days." He got in the van and drove off.

Omar went back inside and just as he was closing the front door, his phone started vibrating. He looked at the phone and saw that he had a text from Zell.

He opened the text and read, "Can you come home? It's important."

He locked the doors, got in his truck and headed home. Whatever was going on, she didn't want to talk about it over the phone. He knew that if something was wrong with one of the kids she would have called him.

He made it home in no time, parked and went inside. When he got inside, Marie's whole family was there talking in rapid Spanish. Marie jumped up crying when she saw him and ran into his arms yelling, "They killed him. They killed him."

"They killed who?" He asked, trying to console her.

"Enrique! They killed Enrique! Those cock sucking cock roaches killed Enrique.

"How did this happen?" Omar asked. Marie was still too distraught to talk so Zell tried to explain.

"From what I gathered from them talking, I think some rival gang shot his car up or the car that he was riding in. I think you can Google it. It's on the internet."

Omar pulled out his phone and Googled latest news from Colombia. A few seconds later, it popped up.

"Billionaire businessman Enrique Santos was killed today when bandits tried to run his car off the road. Several men in black jumped out of several cars and started firing into the car of Santos. His bodyguards immediately returned fire but Enrique and four others were pronounced dead at the scene. Police have no clues to what started the fracas. But they suspect it was an attempted robbery."

Omar looked at the pictures and saw several cars that were so full of bullet holes you couldn't tell what kind of cars they were. Enrique's bodyguards were game but he got caught slipping.

Omar called Glenn and told him what happened and told him to look it up on the internet.

"Damn, look at all those bullet holes in them cars. They had to have been shooting for a pretty good minute," Glenn said.

"I see that shit. I wonder which car he was in?"

"It don't even matter all them hoes shot the fuck up."

"You already know what this means."

"Yeah, when we clear this shit we got right now out, it's over. Everybody should have enough money to live off of the rest of their lives or at least have enough to open some kind of business or something," Glenn said.

"What you plan on doing?"

"Me, Dell, and Jay probably gonna do the same shit you doing. Open some bars or something. We gonna all have to get together and see what kind of family business we can open. Right now we still loaded on this shit he left us."

"Alright, that's cool. You know he left me a house in Florida. I'ma probably go down there and check on the house and shit. I'll let you know before I do anything. Be careful and I'll get back with you later."

"Alright, one."

Omar went back in the room where Marie and her family were and told them, "We all need to talk tonight at 7:00. We will all meet here. I need every one of your people here. I will see you then." He finished up by giving Marie a strong hug.

He went upstairs to find Zell and Shalika. They were in the nursery feeding the girls.

"It's been a stressful day," he said while tickling his daughter's feet. "I'm going to lay down for a few minutes, y'all wanna join me after they go to sleep?"

"Is Marie okay?" Zell asked. "She took Enrique's death kinda hard."

"Oh yeah, I forgot to tell you, that was her brother."

"Marie is Enrique's sister?" Shalika asked before Zell could.

"Yeah. His father had an affair with her mother and he didn't want a scandal about it so he brought her and her mother here. Her mother died several years ago. He told me a week or two ago that this might happen. I told him that Marie and her family would always have a place with us."

"I like Marie and her family," Zell said.

"Me too."

"She's not a legal citizen so I guess that's why he never put anything in her name. He left me a house in Florida. We are gonna have to go down there and check it out eventually."

"I need a vacation and some of that Florida sunshine will do me just fine," Zell replied.

"I almost forgot to tell you, I invited Yolonda over for a few days. She's finished her new sitcom and wanted to get out of Los Angeles for a minute."

"That's fine with me," Omar said. "I'm going to lay down. I'll see y'all in a few."

Chapter 24

"Mr. Omar Wilson, this is Steven Hogan, attorney Steven Hogan, I represent the estate of Enrique Santos and I'm calling to inform you that he left you a home in Palm Springs, Florida, a small yacht and several vehicles. I have transferred the titles to your name. If you can give me a fax number, I will fax all the information to you."

"Okay, here's my fax number," Omar said, giving him his fax number. "I plan to come visit the home in the next week or so."

"Give me a call when you get here and I'll meet you and we can discuss me continuing to handle things for you here in Florida."

"Alright, I'll do that."

"Okay, thank you for your time. I'll see you when you get here."

Omar ended the call. He went downstairs where Zell, Shalika, Em, and J-Low were about to head out the door to go shopping for bathing suits and other stuff they planned to wear while in Florida. He planned on being naked most of his time down there so he didn't need anything new.

They went outside and piled into Zell's Range Rover.

"Let me drive," Em said, taking the keys from Zell.

"In this traffic, you sure can."

They got in and took off. Zell turned the radio on and Kelly Clarkson came from the sound system.

"Hell naw, give me that remote. Let me change that," Shalika said.

"So y'all don't like my choice of music." Zell asked.

"Hell no!" They all responded and burst out laughing.

Shalika turned it to a Kendrick Lamar CD and they all rapped along to the music.

Em noticed that an all-black SUV had gotten behind them right after they turned outta the gates of the house. She switched lanes several times but the SUV continued to follow them. She slowed down and they slowed down. She sped up and they speeded up. She exited off the freeway a couple of exits before the mall.

"Hey, you are taking the wrong exit," Shalika said.

"I know, but I think someone is following us. Don't look back try and look through the rear view mirror. It's that black SUV."

"I see it," J-Low said.

They made a couple of more turns but the SUV stayed behind them, trying to be inconspicuous. But, Em was trained by K-Rock and K-Rock was trained by the Central Intelligence Agency. She knew how to spot a tail.

"Can you see who driving and how many people are in there?" Em asked J-Low.

"Slow down a little and let them get a little closer." She slowed down but the SUV also slowed down.

"How you wanna play it?" J-Low asked.

"Like we were trained. Take they ass out. At least the truck. Shoot the tires out."

"Let's do this shit then," J-Low said.

Em sped up and made several quick turns until she'd lost the SUV. Her and J-Low jumped out and got behind the Range Rover with their weapons trained over the hood in the direction they'd came from.

"Y'all get on the floor," Em told Zell and Shalika.

When the SUV came around the corner, they both opened fire shooting out the two front tires. The SUV jumped the curb and slammed into a tree. They jumped back in the Range Rover and hurried off. Their trip to the mall, forgotten. They hurried home to tell Omar.

When they told Omar, he immediately called Dub, Bobi, D-Money, Robert, and Smurf. They came over and all six of them drove around the neighborhood all night hoping to spot any black SUVs.

After several hours of no luck, they went back to the house. "Whoever it was, they are gone now," Omar said.

"But, nine times outta ten, they'll be back," Em said.

"I wonder who the fuck that could have been," Omar asked nobody in particular, just talking out loud.

"Whoever it was we ain't shooting at no tires no more. I'ma blow they ass away if I see them again," Em said.

Zell and Shalika was shook up not knowing what was going on or who was following them. After everyone had left Omar, Em, J-Low, and K-Rock took turns watching the camera around the property.

Three days before they were scheduled to leave for Florida, Omar got a call.

"This Short Dogg?"

"Yeah, who is this?"

"Hey, my name is Pecas. Rudy Martinez sent me to talk to you. Can you meet me at your club tonight? It's really important."

"Yeah, I'll be at the club around nine. Go to the VIP room. I'ma leave your name at the door."

"Okay it's Pecas and my friend, Chief."

"Alright, I got it."

Omar ended the call and called up his niggas. Thirty minutes later, they were all sitting in his living room. Bobi, D-Money, Dub, Slime, Big Dre, K-Rock, J-Low and Em.

Omar told them about the Mexicans following them to the mall and how he gets a call from some Mexicans that want to talk to him.

"That shit sounds fishy as a muthafucka," Dre said.

"Real talk," Bobi admitted.

"When you gon' meet them niggas?" Dub asked.

"Tonight at the club."

"We all gotta be posted in that bitch tonight," Dub said.

"Look," K-Rock started. "Bobi, D-Money, and Dub. We'll go as couples so we can be seated at the table behind, to the front and side of the table Omar will be at with his company. Big Dre will be the bouncer and Slime you will be behind the bar helping the bartender."

"That sounds like a good plan," Omar said. "Everybody with that?"

They all nodded and gave their approval to the set up. Omar continued, "Then, y'all go get dressed and meet back here in two hours."

***

When the two Mexicans finally showed up, Omar was already sitting at the table. Em and Dub was at the table right behind him. They were both strapped with Drakos. J-Low and D-Money were at the table directly on the other side of him. K-Rock and Bobi sat at the table in front of him. Everybody was strapped with either Drako's or Uzi's. Big Dre was at the door of the VIP room watching everything and Slime was behind the bar.

Omar was surprised when he saw the two Mexicans. They were both about the same height of five foot eight or nine. One was slender and the other one was stocky. What surprised him was that theses weren't no Mexico type Mexicans. These were some niggas from the hood. Their whole demeanor screamed hip hop.

Big Dre walked them over to the table.

"Omar?" When Omar nodded he continued, "I'm Pecas," the stocky one said, "and this is my nigga Chief."

Omar stood up and shook both of their hands. "I'm Omar, have a seat. What y'all drinking?"

"Shit, we Mexicans, Tequila," Chief said and they all laughed.

The waitress brought them a bottle of Patron, an ice bucket and glasses. When she had filled all their cups and walked off, Omar asked, "Now, what y'all needed to see me about?"

"Rudy Martinez sent us. The Colombians are probably going to try and get you back in the game and when you refuse they are gonna come at you."

"The only Colombians I know is dead," Omar said.

"The Santos killed Enrique. You don't know them but they know you. Every hustler in Colombia knows about the young black kid in America that's moving boat loads of product. They want you to work for them," Pecas explained.

"Another thing, Enrique was set up by someone close. Only a few people knew he was in that car and they were waiting for him," Chief said.

"Well, I'm out the game. So if they contact me, I'ma tell them the same thing," Omar said.

"Enrique and Rudy knew you would say that. That's why Enrique instructed Rudy to put the full protection and support of the entire Gonzales Cartel with you," Pecas told him.

Omar was shocked, like damn the shit done got serious. "Y'all really think this shit finna get ugly."

"Real ugly."

"Alright, we'll talk after I come back from Florida. Enrique left me some property up there I gotta go see about."

"Wait til you see it," Chief said, smiling while Pecas nodded.

"Y'all seen it?"

They nodded. "But, back to the real, Rudy will see you in Florida. He gotta holla at you about some more shit."

"Yeah that's cool. This shit getting crazy as fuck. But, if they want it they better bring a bunch of ass."

Chapter 25

They took a private jet from Love Field Airport and landed in Palm Beach. Pecas and Chief met them at the airport when they landed in two black SUVs

"Hey, we meet again," Pecas said.

"What y'all doing down here?" Omar asked after shaking their hands.

"We have been assigned to your personnel protection unit. So wherever you go, we'll be with you." Chief added.

"That's cool with me. Y'all alright with that?" Omar asked.

"Hell yeah. Shit, we get to move around and see some new shit," Pecas answered.

"Well, let's get this show on the road."

They got into the SUVs and drove to the house. When Omar saw the house, he was shocked. The house looked like it took up a whole block. He'd already looked on the internet and seen that the house and property was worth over thirteen million.

The house had twelve bedrooms and fifteen bathrooms, eight fireplaces, a pool house, guest house, servants quarters and a gate house. Ten car garage, pool and a private beach with a private dock and a eighty foot yacht parked at the dock.

They walked around the house looking at the paintings that decorated the walls and checking out the layout. They finally went outside and walked onto the yacht. It was a beautiful black and gold painted boat. The yacht had its own staff, on call twenty four hours a day. They could sit out on the back patio and look upon miles and miles of ocean.

Shalika, Zell, Danielle, Em, K-Rock, J-Low, Shayla, Lil' Omar, Omari, and Omahji were all running around trying to find a room.

"Yolonda just called, she's at the airport," Shalika said coming down the stairs.

Chief drove Shalika and Danielle to the airport to pick her up. Zell put the babies to sleep and they all changed to bathing suits and went outside. Shalika and Yolonda came back about an hour later.

"Hello everybody," Yolonda spoke.

"Hey Yolonda, you have a nice trip," Omar asked.

"Yep, I slept the whole way," she said laughing

"Where everybody at?" Shalika asked.

"Out back on the beach."

"Let's go change and jump in the ocean," Shalika said.

They went upstairs to change. Pecas and Chief told Omar that they all had to go meet Rudy. Omar changed into some shorts and a tee shirt. When he came out the room, he ran right into Yolonda in her bathing suit. Her ass was so fat he instantly got a hard on.

"Damn yo, you look good," he told her.

"Thank you."

"I'ma hit that pussy soon."

"I wish you would hurry up," she whispered and winked at him.

Em, Pecas, Chief and Omar got into one of the SUVs and drove for about twenty minutes before they came to another huge mansion. They drove up to the gate and after a short wait the gate was opened electronically and they drove in, parked and got out. It was several Spanish- looking men standing around when they got out.

"Pecas, Chief, Omar." A tall slender Mexican spoke shaking their hands. "We meet again," he said to Omar.

"We already met?" Omar asked.

"Yeah a long time ago. I met you, you never got a chance to meet me," the man said and him Chief and Pecas started laughing. "I'm Freddy."

"Where did we meet?"

"At the warehouse you robbed. That was a Santos spot you hit and I was watching them. I was in the cut when you pulled up and climbed through the window."

"Naw, you bullshittin me," Omar said.

"We got the whole thing on tape. It was surveillance cameras all over that warehouse."

"Why didn't they come after me? Anyway I checked, wasn't no cameras in that bitch."

"They don't know you hit them. After you left I went in and pulled the tapes. I got the tapes inside. I'll show you."

"You serious, ain't you?"

"Hell yeah. So we watched you to see what you would do with the product," Freddy said as he escorted Omar inside the house. "You set the streets on fire and you handled the work like you had been doing it all your life. You put you a team together and we liked what we saw outta you. Your business was good and you handled it like a real business man. That's why Enrique approached you. We knew you were solid. We had watched you work."

"So, Enrique knew I hit the lick on that warehouse?"

"Hell yeah. You think we would just trust you with that much product without knowing your pedigree? Fuck no! We watched everything you did. What made up our mind about you is when Big Mack did what he did, you were against it. That showed that you had integrity and we loved that. So Enrique decided to take a chance on you and it paid off. You became our number one supplier and you did it without it backfiring on you."

"So all this shit was planned? Enrique didn't just happen to be on the same ship with me by chance?"

"Hell no! You think we'd trust anyone with that much product without knowing something about them. We watched you and made sure that you were the right guy for the job. Plus, Rudy knew you and he spoke highly of you. But we still had to do our investigation."

"Damn this shit gets crazier every day," Omar said.

"You are part of the family now. So whatever you need, just say the word."

He took Omar inside where Rudy was in the back room on the phone. When Rudy finally got off the phone, he greeted Omar with a handshake and a brotherly embrace. Then, he turned and hugged Em.

"We gotta talk. We know who set Enrique up and the same person informed The Santos that you are here in Palm Beach. You have a rat inside your circle," Rudy said.

"Are you positive? I'm almost positive I can vouch for my people. Who do you think it is?"

"We know who it is for sure. We have recorded phone conversations. Listen to this," Rudy said pushing the play button on a mini recorder.

'Enrique will be spending the weekend at the country villa. He will leave tomorrow afternoon. Nobody but a few people know he's going.' The female voice said.

Omar looked over at Em and Em looked at him. They both knew that voice immediately.

"Dirty bitch," Omar whispered.

"That's not all, check this out."

'Omar will be in Florida this week. He's coming to check on the house that Enrique left him.'

It was the same voice and they both recognized the voice again. Omar was crushed. He hated rats but the betrayal was what really got to him.

"We have people in position to take care of this ASAP," Rudy told him while Freddy looked on.

"Naw, I exterminate my own residence. This is personal, I gotta handle this myself."

They both nodded understanding how he felt. Then Freddy said, "It's always someone close to you that you'd least expect. Don't let this ruin your trip here. Enjoy the sunshine, take the yacht out on the ocean."

"Yeah, I will."

"We expect the Santos to try and make contact with you while you are down here. Nothing violent at first, just a meeting to try and get you working for them. But, when you refuse, that's when the fun starts," Freddy said.

"They might as well get ready to rumble. Cause I'm retired."

"Well we are ready for whatever they try and pull," Rudy assured him.

They sit around talking and Freddy showed him the old tape of him robbing the warehouse and just like he said there were cameras all over the place.

Freddy thought that it was hilarious that a black kid from the streets would have the balls to even attempt to hit a lick on the cartel.

"Old man Santos was one mad bastard when they told him the place had been cleaned out. When he found out the tapes were missing, he figured that one of his own men did it. Every son of a bitch who couldn't verify their whereabouts that night, got smoked," Freddy said laughing.

"No shit?" Omar asked.

"Hell yeah! The old man was fit to be tied. He couldn't understand what happened to the tapes."

Later, after they returned to the house, Omar got Em, J-Low and K-Rock together and they discussed the betrayal and tried to come up with a remedy to resolve it.

Once they came up with a plan that he was satisfied with, they went and changed and joined everyone else on the beach.

Chapter 26

Em sat on the plane on her way back to Dallas. She closed her eyes and tried to get a nap in but couldn't sleep. She kept thinking about the snake in their midst. She remembered the look on Omar's face when he recognized the voice on the tape Rudy played for him.

Em was in love with Omar. She admitted that to herself. She knew his situation and knew that she would never have him all to herself. But, that wasn't the kind of relationship she wanted.

She was in love with K-Rock and J-Low also. The time she spent with Omar was enough for her. Their weekly arrangement was fine with her. She loved the tenderness and affection her girls gave and showed her. But, a woman needed a man every now and then to put her fire out.

Omar was very attentive and he listened to their opinions and took care of the house the way a man was supposed to. He was generous and made sure they never wanted for anything. That's why she would lay her life down for him.

When the plane finally landed, she got her small bag and took an Uber to the house. Marie met her at the door.

"Hey Em, where's everybody else?" She asked.

"They are still in Florida. I had to come back and get some paperwork. I'm headed back up there tonight."

"Oh, okay. You need any help with anything?"

"Naw, I'm good."

"Okay, holler if you need me," Marie said walking off.

Em went to her room and pulled out her bag. She made three bombs and put timers on them. When she was done, she came out and looked around to see if Marie was still in the house. When she saw the coast was clear, she went from room to room handling her business. An hour later, she was done and on her way back to the airport. She got on the plane and was asleep before the plane took off.

At seven p.m., Omar had Marie's entire family in the basement talking to them on the safe phone.

"Marie, I can't believe that you would set up your own brother and try to set me up. Don't deny it because the phones are bugged and I just listened to all the recordings. I heard you tell them that I would be coming to Florida and I heard you tell them that Enrique was on his way to the villa in the country. I just wanted you and your family to know that," Omar said before he hung up the phone.

Sixty seconds later, the entire house was rocked by a huge explosion, instantly killing everyone in the house. He got a call from the security people telling him about the explosion.

"Mr. Wilson, I'm sorry to inform you that your home exploded about an hour ago. The police and firemen are still there but we don't think there are any survivors."

"Do they know what caused the explosion?" He asked.

"They think it was a gas line leak. I will call you when I have more information."

"Okay, thank you."

"Oh yeah, I almost forgot, there were two survivors. Your two puppies were running around outside. They are safe and unharmed."

"Thank you," he said before ending the call. He sat back and fired up a huge blunt, thinking to himself, 'Marie was a rat bitch.'

He was back in Short Dogg mode. "Now," he whispered, "Let's get at these Santos muthafuckas."

The end.

140

COMING SOON

The Lane 3

Lock Down Publications and Ca$h Presents
Assisted Publishing Packages

BASIC PACKAGE $499 Editing Cover Design Formatting	UPGRADED PACKAGE $800 Typing Editing Cover Design Formatting
ADVANCE PACKAGE $1,200 Typing Editing Cover Design Formatting Copyright registration Proofreading Upload book to Amazon	LDP SUPREME PACKAGE $1,500 Typing Editing Cover Design Formatting Copyright registration Proofreading Set up Amazon account Upload book to Amazon Advertise on LDP, Amazon and Facebook Page

***Other services available upon request.
Additional charges may apply

Lock Down Publications
P.O. Box 944
Stockbridge, GA 30281-9998
Phone: 470 303-9761

Submission Guideline

Submit the first three chapters of your completed manuscript to ldpsubmissions@gmail.com. In the subject line add **Your Book's Title**. The manuscript must be in a Word Doc file and sent as an attachment. Document should be in Times New Roman, double spaced, and in size 12 font. Also, provide your synopsis and full contact information. If sending multiple submissions, they must each be in a separate email.

Have a story but no way to send it electronically? You can still submit to LDP/Ca$h Presents. Send in the first three chapters, written or typed, of your completed manuscript to:

LDP: Submissions Dept
P.O. Box 944
Stockbridge, GA 30281-9998

DO NOT send original manuscript. Must be a duplicate. Provide your synopsis and a cover letter containing your full contact information.

Thanks for considering LDP and Ca$h Presents.

NEW RELEASES

BLOODLINE OF A SAVAGE **BY PRINCE A. TAUHID**

THE MURDER QUEENS 4 **BY MICHAEL GALLON**

THE BUTTERFLY MAFIA **BY FUMIYA PAYNE**

KING KILLA 2 **BY VINCENT "VITTO" HOLLOWAY**

BABY, I'M WINTERTIME COLD 3 **BY MEESHA**

THESE VICIOUS STREETS **BY PRINCE A. TAUHID**

TIL DEATH 2 **BY ARYANNA**

CITY OF SMOKE 2 **BY MOLOTTI**

STEPPERS **BY KING RIO**

THE LANE **BY KEN-KEN SPENCE**

MONEY GAME 2 **BY SMOOVE DOLLA**

THE BLACK DIAMOND CARTEL **BY SAYNOMORE**

CRIME BOSS 2 **BY PLAYA RAY**

THUG OF SPADES **BY COREY ROBINSON**

LOVE IN THE TRENCHES 2 **BY COREY ROBINSON**

TIL DEATH 3 **BY ARYANNA**

THE BIRTH OF A GANGSTER 4 **BY DELMONT PLAYER**

PRODUCT OF THE STREETS **BY DEMOND "MONEY" ANDERSON**

Coming Soon from Lock Down Publications/Ca$h Presents

BLOOD OF A BOSS VI
SHADOWS OF THE GAME II
TRAP BASTARD II
By **Askari**

LOYAL TO THE GAME IV
By **T.J. & Jelissa**

TRUE SAVAGE VIII
MIDNIGHT CARTEL IV
DOPE BOY MAGIC IV
CITY OF KINGZ III
NIGHTMARE ON SILENT AVE II
THE PLUG OF LIL MEXICO II
CLASSIC CITY II
By **Chris Green**

BLAST FOR ME III
A SAVAGE DOPEBOY III
CUTTHROAT MAFIA III
DUFFLE BAG CARTEL VII
HEARTLESS GOON VI
By **Ghost**

A HUSTLER'S DECEIT III
KILL ZONE II
BAE BELONGS TO ME III
TIL DEATH II
By **Aryanna**

KING OF THE TRAP III
By **T.J. Edwards**

GORILLAZ IN THE BAY V
3X KRAZY III
STRAIGHT BEAST MODE III
By **De'Kari**

KINGPIN KILLAZ IV
STREET KINGS III
PAID IN BLOOD III
CARTEL KILLAZ IV
DOPE GODS III
By **Hood Rich**

SINS OF A HUSTLA II
By **ASAD**

YAYO V
BRED IN THE GAME 2
By **S. Allen**

THE STREETS WILL TALK II
By **Yolanda Moore**

SON OF A DOPE FIEND III
HEAVEN GOT A GHETTO III
SKI MASK MONEY III
By **Renta**

LOYALTY AIN'T PROMISED III
By **Keith Williams**

I'M NOTHING WITHOUT HIS LOVE II
SINS OF A THUG II
TO THE THUG I LOVED BEFORE II
IN A HUSTLER I TRUST II
By **Monet Dragun**

QUIET MONEY IV
EXTENDED CLIP III
THUG LIFE IV
By **Trai'Quan**

THE STREETS MADE ME IV
By **Larry D. Wright**

IF YOU CROSS ME ONCE III
ANGEL V
By **Anthony Fields**

THE STREETS WILL NEVER CLOSE IV
By **K'ajji**

HARD AND RUTHLESS III
KILLA KOUNTY IV
By **Khufu**

MONEY GAME III
By **Smoove Dolla**

MURDA WAS THE CASE III
Elijah R. Freeman

AN UNFORESEEN LOVE IV
BABY, I'M WINTERTIME COLD III
By **Meesha**

QUEEN OF THE ZOO III
By **Black Migo**

CONFESSIONS OF A JACKBOY III
By **Nicholas Lock**

JACK BOYS VS DOPE BOYS IV
A GANGSTA'S QUR'AN V
COKE GIRLZ II
COKE BOYS II
LIFE OF A SAVAGE V
CHI'RAQ GANGSTAS V
SOSA GANG III
BRONX SAVAGES II
BODYMORE KINGPINS II
By **Romell Tukes**

KING KILLA II
By **Vincent "Vitto" Holloway**

BETRAYAL OF A THUG III
By **Fre$h**

THE MURDER QUEENS III
By **Michael Gallon**

THE BIRTH OF A GANGSTER III
By **Delmont Player**

TREAL LOVE II
By **Le'Monica Jackson**

FOR THE LOVE OF BLOOD III
By **Jamel Mitchell**

RAN OFF ON DA PLUG II
By **Paper Boi Rari**

HOOD CONSIGLIERE III
By **Keese**

PRETTY GIRLS DO NASTY THINGS II
By **Nicole Goosby**

PROTÉGÉ OF A LEGEND III
LOVE IN THE TRENCHES II
By **Corey Robinson**

IT'S JUST ME AND YOU II
By **Ah'Million**

FOREVER GANGSTA III
By **Adrian Dulan**

GORILLAZ IN THE TRENCHES II
By **SayNoMore**

THE COCAINE PRINCESS VIII
By **King Rio**

CRIME BOSS II
By **Playa Ray**

LOYALTY IS EVERYTHING III
By **Molotti**

HERE TODAY GONE TOMORROW II
By **Fly Rock**

THE LANE 2 | KEN-KEN SPENCE

REAL G'S MOVE IN SILENCE II
By **Von Diesel**

GRIMEY WAYS IV
By **Ray Vinci**

Available Now

RESTRAINING ORDER I & II
By **CA$H & Coffee**

LOVE KNOWS NO BOUNDARIES I II & III
By **Coffee**

RAISED AS A GOON I, II, III & IV
BRED BY THE SLUMS I, II, III
BLAST FOR ME I & II
ROTTEN TO THE CORE I II III
A BRONX TALE I, II, III
DUFFLE BAG CARTEL I II III IV V VI
HEARTLESS GOON I II III IV V
A SAVAGE DOPEBOY I II
DRUG LORDS I II III
CUTTHROAT MAFIA I II
KING OF THE TRENCHES
By **Ghost**

LAY IT DOWN I & II
LAST OF A DYING BREED I II
BLOOD STAINS OF A SHOTTA I & II III
By **Jamaica**

LOYAL TO THE GAME I II III
LIFE OF SIN I, II III
By **TJ & Jelissa**

IF LOVING HIM IS WRONG…I & II
LOVE ME EVEN WHEN IT HURTS I II III
By **Jelissa**

THE LANE 2 | KEN-KEN SPENCE

BLOODY COMMAS I & II
SKI MASK CARTEL I, II & III
KING OF NEW YORK I II, III IV V
RISE TO POWER I II III
COKE KINGS I II III IV V
BORN HEARTLESS I II III IV
KING OF THE TRAP I II
By **T.J. Edwards**

WHEN THE STREETS CLAP BACK I & II III
THE HEART OF A SAVAGE I II III IV
MONEY MAFIA I II
LOYAL TO THE SOIL I II III
By **Jibril Williams**

A DISTINGUISHED THUG STOLE MY HEART I II &
III
LOVE SHOULDN'T HURT I II III IV
RENEGADE BOYS I II III IV
PAID IN KARMA I II III
SAVAGE STORMS I II III
AN UNFORESEEN LOVE I II III
BABY, I'M WINTERTIME COLD I II
By **Meesha**

A GANGSTER'S CODE I &, II III
A GANGSTER'S SYN I II III
THE SAVAGE LIFE I II III
CHAINED TO THE STREETS I II III
BLOOD ON THE MONEY I II III
A GANGSTA'S PAIN I II III
By **J-Blunt**

PUSH IT TO THE LIMIT
By **Bre' Hayes**

BLOOD OF A BOSS I, II, III, IV, V
SHADOWS OF THE GAME
TRAP BASTARD
By **Askari**

THE STREETS BLEED MURDER I, II & III
THE HEART OF A GANGSTA I II& III
By **Jerry Jackson**

CUM FOR ME I II III IV V VI VII VIII
An **LDP Erotica Collaboration**

BRIDE OF A HUSTLA I II & II
THE FETTI GIRLS I, II& III
CORRUPTED BY A GANGSTA I, II III, IV
BLINDED BY HIS LOVE
THE PRICE YOU PAY FOR LOVE I, II ,III
DOPE GIRL MAGIC I II III
By **Destiny Skai**

WHEN A GOOD GIRL GOES BAD
By **Adrienne**

A GANGSTER'S REVENGE I II III & IV
THE BOSS MAN'S DAUGHTERS I II III IV V
A SAVAGE LOVE I & II
BAE BELONGS TO ME I II
A HUSTLER'S DECEIT I, II, III
WHAT BAD BITCHES DO I, II, III
SOUL OF A MONSTER I II III
KILL ZONE
A DOPE BOY'S QUEEN I II III
TIL DEATH
By **Aryanna**

THE COST OF LOYALTY I II III
By Kweli

A KINGPIN'S AMBITION
A KINGPIN'S AMBITION **II**
I MURDER FOR THE DOUGH
By **Ambitious**

TRUE SAVAGE I II III IV V VI VII
DOPE BOY MAGIC I, II, III
MIDNIGHT CARTEL I II III
CITY OF KINGZ I II
NIGHTMARE ON SILENT AVE
THE PLUG OF LIL MEXICO II
CLASSIC CITY
By **Chris Green**

A DOPEBOY'S PRAYER
By **Eddie "Wolf" Lee**

THE KING CARTEL I, II & III
By **Frank Gresham**

THESE NIGGAS AIN'T LOYAL I, II & III
By **Nikki Tee**

GANGSTA SHYT I II &III
By **CATO**

THE ULTIMATE BETRAYAL
By **Phoenix**

BOSS'N UP I, II & III
By **Royal Nicole**

THE LANE 2 | KEN-KEN SPENCE

I LOVE YOU TO DEATH
By **Destiny J**

I RIDE FOR MY HITTA
I STILL RIDE FOR MY HITTA
By **Misty Holt**

LOVE & CHASIN' PAPER
By **Qay Crockett**

TO DIE IN VAIN
SINS OF A HUSTLA
By **ASAD**

BROOKLYN HUSTLAZ
By **Boogsy Morina**

BROOKLYN ON LOCK I & II
By **Sonovia**

GANGSTA CITY
By **Teddy Duke**

A DRUG KING AND HIS DIAMOND I & II III
A DOPEMAN'S RICHES
HER MAN, MINE'S TOO I, II
CASH MONEY HO'S
THE WIFEY I USED TO BE I II
PRETTY GIRLS DO NASTY THINGS
By Nicole Goosby

LIPSTICK KILLAH I, II, III
CRIME OF PASSION I II & III
FRIEND OR FOE I II III
By **Mimi**

TRAPHOUSE KING I II & III
KINGPIN KILLAZ I II III
STREET KINGS I II
PAID IN BLOOD I II
CARTEL KILLAZ I II III
DOPE GODS I II
By **Hood Rich**

STEADY MOBBN' I, II, III
THE STREETS STAINED MY SOUL I II III
By **Marcellus Allen**

WHO SHOT YA I, II, III
SON OF A DOPE FIEND I II
HEAVEN GOT A GHETTO I II
SKI MASK MONEY I II
By **Renta**

GORILLAZ IN THE BAY I II III IV
TEARS OF A GANGSTA I II
3X KRAZY I II
STRAIGHT BEAST MODE I II
By **DE'KARI**

TRIGGADALE I II III
MURDA WAS THE CASE I II
By **Elijah R. Freeman**

THE STREETS ARE CALLING
By **Duquie Wilson**

SLAUGHTER GANG I II III
RUTHLESS HEART I II III
By **Willie Slaughter**

THE LANE 2 | KEN-KEN SPENCE

GOD BLESS THE TRAPPERS I, II, III
THESE SCANDALOUS STREETS I, II, III
FEAR MY GANGSTA I, II, III IV, V
THESE STREETS DON'T LOVE NOBODY I, II
BURY ME A G I, II, III, IV, V
A GANGSTA'S EMPIRE I, II, III, IV
THE DOPEMAN'S BODYGAURD I II
THE REALEST KILLAZ I II III
THE LAST OF THE OGS I II III
By **Tranay Adams**

MARRIED TO A BOSS I II III
By **Destiny Skai & Chris Green**

KINGZ OF THE GAME I II III IV V VI VII
CRIME BOSS
By **Playa Ray**

FUK SHYT
By **Blakk Diamond**

DON'T F#CK WITH MY HEART I II
By **Linnea**

ADDICTED TO THE DRAMA I II III
IN THE ARM OF HIS BOSS II
By **Jamila**

YAYO I II III IV
A SHOOTER'S AMBITION I II
BRED IN THE GAME
By **S. Allen**

LOYALTY AIN'T PROMISED I II
By **Keith Williams**

157

THE LANE 2 | KEN-KEN SPENCE

TRAP GOD I II III
RICH $AVAGE I II III
MONEY IN THE GRAVE I II III
By **Martell Troublesome Bolden**

FOREVER GANGSTA I II
GLOCKS ON SATIN SHEETS I II
By **Adrian Dulan**

TOE TAGZ I II III IV
LEVELS TO THIS SHYT I II
IT'S JUST ME AND YOU
By **Ah'Million**

KINGPIN DREAMS I II III
RAN OFF ON DA PLUG
By **Paper Boi Rari**

CONFESSIONS OF A GANGSTA I II III IV
CONFESSIONS OF A JACKBOY I II
By **Nicholas Lock**

I'M NOTHING WITHOUT HIS LOVE
SINS OF A THUG
TO THE THUG I LOVED BEFORE
A GANGSTA SAVED XMAS
IN A HUSTLER I TRUST
By **Monet Dragun**

QUIET MONEY I II III
THUG LIFE I II III
EXTENDED CLIP I II
A GANGSTA'S PARADISE
By **Trai'Quan**

THE LANE 2 | KEN-KEN SPENCE

CAUGHT UP IN THE LIFE I II III
THE STREETS NEVER LET GO I II III
By **Robert Baptiste**

NEW TO THE GAME I II III
MONEY, MURDER & MEMORIES I II III
By **Malik D. Rice**

CREAM I II III
THE STREETS WILL TALK
By **Yolanda Moore**

LIFE OF A SAVAGE I II III IV
A GANGSTA'S QUR'AN I II III IV
MURDA SEASON I II III
GANGLAND CARTEL I II III
CHI'RAQ GANGSTAS I II III IV
KILLERS ON ELM STREET I II III
JACK BOYZ N DA BRONX I II III
A DOPEBOY'S DREAM I II III
JACK BOYS VS DOPE BOYS I II III
COKE GIRLZ
COKE BOYS
SOSA GANG I II
BRONX SAVAGES
BODYMORE KINGPINS
By **Romell Tukes**

THE STREETS MADE ME I II III
By **Larry D. Wright**

CONCRETE KILLA I II III
VICIOUS LOYALTY I II III
By **Kingpen**

THE ULTIMATE SACRIFICE I, II, III, IV, V, VI
KHADIFI
IF YOU CROSS ME ONCE I II
ANGEL I II III IV
IN THE BLINK OF AN EYE
By **Anthony Fields**

THE LIFE OF A HOOD STAR
By **Ca$h & Rashia Wilson**

THE STREETS WILL NEVER CLOSE I II III
By **K'ajji**

NIGHTMARES OF A HUSTLA I II III
By **King Dream**

HARD AND RUTHLESS I II
MOB TOWN 251
THE BILLIONAIRE BENTLEYS I II III
REAL G'S MOVE IN SILENCE
By **Von Diesel**

GHOST MOB
By **Stilloan Robinson**

MOB TIES I II III IV V VI
SOUL OF A HUSTLER, HEART OF A KILLER I II
GORILLAZ IN THE TRENCHES
By **SayNoMore**

BODYMORE MURDERLAND I II III
THE BIRTH OF A GANGSTER I II
By **Delmont Player**

THE LANE 2 | KEN-KEN SPENCE

FOR THE LOVE OF A BOSS
By **C. D. Blue**

KILLA KOUNTY I II III IV
By Khufu

MOBBED UP I II III IV
THE BRICK MAN I II III IV V
THE COCAINE PRINCESS I II III IV V VI VII
By **King Rio**

MONEY GAME I II
By **Smoove Dolla**

A GANGSTA'S KARMA I II III
By **FLAME**

KING OF THE TRENCHES I II III
By **GHOST & TRANAY ADAMS**

QUEEN OF THE ZOO I II
By **Black Migo**

GRIMEY WAYS I II III
By **Ray Vinci**

XMAS WITH AN ATL SHOOTER
By **Ca$h & Destiny Skai**

KING KILLA
By **Vincent "Vitto" Holloway**

BETRAYAL OF A THUG I II
By **Fre$h**

THE LANE 2 | KEN-KEN SPENCE

THE MURDER QUEENS I II
By **Michael Gallon**

TREAL LOVE
By **Le'Monica Jackson**

FOR THE LOVE OF BLOOD I II
By **Jamel Mitchell**

HOOD CONSIGLIERE I II
By **Keese**

PROTÉGÉ OF A LEGEND I II
LOVE IN THE TRENCHES
By **Corey Robinson**

BORN IN THE GRAVE I II III
By **Self Made Tay**

MOAN IN MY MOUTH
By **XTASY**

TORN BETWEEN A GANGSTER AND A
GENTLEMAN
By **J-BLUNT & Miss Kim**

LOYALTY IS EVERYTHING I II
By **Molotti**

HERE TODAY GONE TOMORROW
By **Fly Rock**

PILLOW PRINCESS
By **S. Hawkins**

THE LANE 2 | KEN-KEN SPENCE

SANCTIFIED AND HORNY
by **XTASY**

THE PLUG OF LIL MEXICO 2
by **CHRIS GREEN**

THE BLACK DIAMOND CARTEL
by **SAYNOMORE**

THE BIRTH OF A GANGSTER 3
by **DELMONT PLAYER**

BOOKS BY LDP'S CEO, CA$H

TRUST IN NO MAN
TRUST IN NO MAN 2
TRUST IN NO MAN 3
BONDED BY BLOOD
SHORTY GOT A THUG
THUGS CRY
THUGS CRY 2
THUGS CRY 3
TRUST NO BITCH
TRUST NO BITCH 2
TRUST NO BITCH 3
TIL MY CASKET DROPS
RESTRAINING ORDER
RESTRAINING ORDER 2
IN LOVE WITH A CONVICT
LIFE OF A HOOD STAR
XMAS WITH AN ATL SHOOTER